LOVE IN HER BIG TWO-HEARTED RIVER

PAUL MICHAEL PETERS

CONTENTS

Ebook: 979-8-9902614-4-0

Paperback: 979-8-9902614-5-7

Hardback: 979-8-9902614-6-4

To my faithful companion, Perri Winkleberry, for your unconditional love. A good cat.

FOREWORD

Michigan's Upper Peninsula is the location of one of my favorite day trip destinations, the Toonerville Trolley & Riverboat Tour to Tahquamenon Falls. A thirty-five-minute narrow gauge rail, affectionately known as the Toonerville Trolley (a nickname derived from a popular 1930s comic strip), takes you to a boat that runs up and down the Tahquamenon River. In my lifetime, the riverboat was the Hiawatha, named in honor of the Native American leader made famous in Longfellow's popular story. It replaced the Paul Bunyan years prior to my first journey.

During the two-hour trip to the falls and back, the captain shares stories about the river, the woods, history, and science, helping passengers understand and appreciate this special place in the world. On the top deck, photographers with a keen eye can capture the vibrant wildlife, including a large variety of birds and mammals along the river's edge. I loved every trip taken on that boat, on that river, learning from that captain.

On one particularly memorable trip, before the captain retired, a kind family adopted me for the day. As a single traveler, it's very nice to meet and talk with others, to hear their stories. After a glorious six-hour journey, as we walked from the train to the parking lot, the daughter remarked that these goodbyes were the most difficult part. They were headed in the opposite direction from me before returning home to Petoskey, with their destination being Pictured Rocks National Lakeshore, which would take them through the town of Seney.

While goodbyes are never easy, I found myself thinking about the family and their journey for the rest of that trip. It was a journey similar to the one Ernest Hemingway took when returning home from the war in Europe. For Hemingway, it was about healing. This region has always had medicinal powers for me, so I can clearly understand what a good fishing trip in solitude can do for the spirit and mind.

On a subsequent trip later that summer, with Hemingway and that family on my mind, I drove to the Two Hearted River. Near Pine Stump Junction, the perfect place for lunch after a morning on snowmobiles, the river flows close to a road that, with the help of GPS, you can follow to where the river meets Lake Superior. This trail is nowhere near Hemingway's fishing trip on the Fox River near Seney, but as he said, the title of this story of redemption is about poetry.

Those two trips north were the inspiration for this novella, its characters, and its themes. I have tried to capture the things I love about this land, so please excuse me if I go on a bit too long in places, attempting to capture that enchantment.

As you embark on this literary journey through "Love in her Big Two-Hearted River," I invite you to immerse yourself in the beauty and healing power of Michigan's Upper Peninsula, to experience the connections we make along the way, and to discover the transformative potential of self-reflection amidst nature's embrace.

Cozy up by the fire, find your reading nook, and escape your troubles.

LOVE IN HER BIG TWO-HEARTED RIVER

1

"The Prospector 14, it's your canoe. No doubt," Billy said with a smile, leaning against the wooden counter of the outfitter's store. "I'm sorry, what did you say your name was?"

"Sonny."

"A perfect name to captain the Prospector 14."

It was her first time stepping into the store—a cozy haven channeling the rustic charm of a backwoods cottage, where friends gathered for hours of card-playing after idyllic days by the lake or among nature's wonders. The aged and meticulously crafted timber ceiling captivated, while the salesman, towering at six foot two with a sturdy frame forged by a lifetime of wilderness adventures, exuded kindness and patience. The outfitter's product was a vision. It said, "Welcome to this beautiful retreat, where cherished moments and warm camaraderie intertwine amidst the wilderness-inspired ambiance."

Sonny raised her eyebrows, looking skeptical. "But how do you know?" she asked. "All these canoes look the same."

"Each one of these canoes serves a unique purpose," he said. "You're traveling alone?"

She nodded.

"Well then, that eliminates all the tandems. Tandems make up about eighty percent of what's in front of you. You want something you can manage and carry by yourself," he explained. "You'll be gone for several days?"

"Yes, a week," she replied.

"So you need a canoe that can carry the weight of everything you're bringing," Billy continued. "And from your questions, I gather you're not, what one might call, an experienced traveler." His toothy grin grew. "But I spend every day thinking about canoeing and water travel. If I had the means and the wherewithal, this would be the canoe I'd choose for myself—the Swift Prospector 14. It's the one you not only want but need. Especially when you need to portage; the light weight will make it easy to carry."

"Portage?" she asked.

"With a block in the river, if you can't get over it, you put the canoe on your back and carry it over land, around the block."

"What blocks rivers?"

"Trees, branches, brush—anything brought downriver. You'll need a saw."

"A saw?"

"Hand saw. We carry those," Billy said, pointing to a display. "Have you canoed before?"

"In scouts. On a lake," she replied.

"So it's been a few years," he said. "Which river are you traveling?"

"The Two-Hearted," she replied.

"Ah, that's a challenge," Billy said, his eyes squinting, then opening with excitement. "An equipment challenge. And the Swift Prospector 14 is the equipment you need to get started. It'll keep you upright in the rapids and be light as a feather when you lift it up. The only heavy thing on your trip will be your baggage."

He looked out of the window and saw her white minivan parked outside. Reliable, all-wheel drive, it was the perfect suburban vehicle. But it was no match for the wild north. "What else will you be needing for your expedition?" he asked.

"Everything," she said.

He grinned. "Very exciting," he said. "Very exciting indeed."

Sonny spent four hours with Billy, the outfitter. He was patient and kind, guiding her through every piece of gear she would need for her journey. She packed her food, dry clothing, sleep system, maps, and GPS into a red 30-liter dry-bag. A tight fit into the canoe, it would balance her weight on the moving waters. Billy even gave her a second maple angled paddle for cuts and turns at no charge. Her first paddle had a big fat face, which would give her more "umph" in every stroke. "The difference between 'try' and 'triumph' is a little more umph," Billy said.

"It will look beautiful strapped to the top of your Honda Odyssey." Billy showed her where to tie the canoe straps. He instructed how to keep them taut, how to loosen them, and what to look for before getting on the road. As she turned out of the parking lot and onto the main road, the orange safety straps flapped outside the windshield, like inflatables outside car dealerships. The fun of the distraction ended when she pulled into her driveway.

Her house had looked dark and empty ever since Mitch died, even in the late afternoon. The lawn... she remembered Mitch spraying the girls with the water hose on the lawn while they ran through sprinklers in the summer. He spent weeks each year walking back and forth behind the mower just to make the lawn look right. She would have to learn how to do that now. There were so many things she would have to learn to do alone.

The garage door opened with a click of the button. Sonny started to roll in, but the dancing orange ribbon caught her attention. Sonny slammed hard on the brakes. Her seat belt tightened and jerked her forward. She watched the Prospector 14 shoot past the windshield in a green flash, taking flight and breaking the orange strap. The vessel took a bounce off the cement garage floor and slid four feet before friction brought it to a stop. Putting the Honda in park, she leaned forward in disbelief. Her brand new, five-thousand-dollar Kevlar fiber investment had been only an inch away from total destruction. Hitting the concrete steps at full speed would have shattered it. She sighed, disappointed in herself for daydreaming and not thinking things through. "Oh, Mitch," she said to the spirits. "You would have laughed at me pretty hard if you were here."

She backed up the Honda, then got into Mitch's Toyota Tundra and moved it parallel to the minivan on the drive apron. "Billy was right," she said out loud, lifting the Prospector over her head as she had practiced in the store. "It's light as a feather." Cautious, she took the Prospector to the back of the Tundra. Placing it in the bed, it seemed less likely to take flight. Her new pack went into the second door of the cab behind the driver.

Before first light, she would set out. The drive would take her five hours north to the Mackinac Bridge. In another ninety minutes, to Newberry, where she planned to spend the night. The next day she would find the drop-off point on the river, avoiding a nighttime search. Lumber truck trails and sandy winding two-tracks were how most roads in the north woods looked. It took a clear and rested mind to navigate. Taking on the river was not a task for the light-hearted.

"This is a bold new venture," she admitted to Mitch. "It's a reasonable risk, not like bullfighting or safari. It's canoeing. I did this as a brownie and a scout. How hard can it be?"

Sonny went back into the garage. She inspected her bicycle hanging upside down from the rafter. Mitch had hung it there years earlier to "save space." Digging through the organized bike storage, she found the red metal box for pumping tires. Attaching the nozzle and reading the psi on the tire wall, she clicked until the number on the box matched. It started with a whir and buzz. It lasted about 90 seconds then shut itself off. She did the same for the rear tire. Then she did the old thumb test, pressing and feeling it as if she knew what to expect. The thick knobby tires reminded her of unfulfilled promises. They had purchased them to go mountain biking. Not some extreme sport of masochistic mountainside descent, but slow, light rides in the park.

As she walked the bike to the rear of Mitch's Toyota, her daughter pulled into the driveway. She drove a white VW Atlas that showed the rarity of a visit to the car wash.

"Mom," Evanora called as she got out. "Did you cut your hair?"

"I did."

Evanora exited and walked over to give her mother a hug. "It's short. I like it." She gave a closer inspection to the hairdo. In her hands, she presented her mother a clear plastic container with a snap lid and Evanora's name handwritten in black ink on a piece of white tape stuck to the side. Inside was warm lasagna that would take her mother more than a week to consume on her own.

"Thank you," Sonny said as she accepted the dish and placed it in the back of the truck bed.

"You look tired. Did you get any sleep?"

"Not for years."

"What are you doing?"

"Going on a trip."

"Did you rob a bank or something? Trying to get away?"

"Not exactly, just going on a trip."

The two boys had already let themselves out of the back of the Atlas and were running across the yard. Spring meant mud, and it clung to the boys in little splattered clumps with each step. Sonny could already see the colors from dead leaves mushing into their blue jeans. This was their mother's problem, not hers.

"I can see that, Mom. Where? When? What are you going to do?" Evanora pestered.

"It's a canoe trip. I'm going on a canoe trip."

"Oh. With whom?"

"Myself, me, I."

"And where? Where are you going?"

"It's up north. I'll email you and your sister the details tonight to let you know where I'm going and when to expect me back."

"This seems rather sudden. It's only been a week since

the funeral. Why the sudden urge to canoe? I don't remember you saying anything about canoeing last week."

"Your mother needs to get away for a while, get some fresh air."

"Are you OK? Is everything OK? You know we can talk."

"Everything is fine, just adding a little adventure to my life." Sonny reached into the back of the truck. She had to stretch to reach the water bottle still in the holder on the bike frame. "This might come off; might as well keep it with me."

"What if I hadn't swung by with the boys? Were you going to go without a word?"

"I said I was going to email you and your sister."

"So, Glinda doesn't know? Canoe—it's, well, not what I would have expected. Don't you have to camp for that? Or do they have cabins on the river? Is it a river?"

"It's on a river, and there are no cabins. I'm camping."

"A tent? You're camping? Do you have a tent? A sleeping bag?"

Sonny stepped to the rear door of Mitch's truck and pointed to the red dry-bag and blue barrel Billy sold her. "Check, and check."

"What about food and water?"

"This is a water filter; rivers are made of the stuff. You just filter through here and it's safe. The outfitter sold me a barrel of food packs. I'm set."

"You know you have to be in decent shape to do something like that—you need to know how to do stuff and things to survive."

"They covered stuff and things in the scouts. I have a badge for both, and another badge for odds and ends. Would you like me to dig up my sash? I was the troop leader for you and your sister."

"Yeah, but Mom, scouts? Is that the resume you're going with on this trip? You might as well have said you watched a YouTube video, and that's all you needed."

"YouTube, good idea. I'll do that tonight while I write you and your sister an email."

"Mom." Evanora shook her head.

"Evanora." She mocked her tone and inflection. "What's your point? You're implying I'm old and out of shape? I don't have the smarts for some time in the backwoods?"

All sheepish, Evanora replied, "Well, no."

"Your father and I talked about getting out and trying new things. I didn't want to wait another season. I decided to go. I've been prepping all morning with an expert."

"Going today?"

"In the morning. Tomorrow morning."

"Who will watch the house?" Evanora asked.

"The house will be fine. Don't worry about the mail. The advertisements and coupons will pile up and be here for me when I get back."

Sonny closed the door of the truck cab. She tightened the

final strap and went back to the Honda to grab her purse and things to move them to the truck.

"You'll send me an email with the details?" Evanora asked.

"Yes, I will send you an email with ALL the details, Evanora. I'll have my cell phone if you need me."

"Does Glinda know?"

"No. I said that. Your sister doesn't know," Sonny said. A small smile of superiority crept across her daughter's face. Even as adults, the two were still siblings who knew how to push each other's buttons.

"Boys!" Evanora called. "Where did they go? Boys!"

The two came around the corner at full speed, caked in mud from the creek in Sonny's backyard. The Atlas was perfect for situations like this. The plastic-covered seats make for easy cleaning. The boys were like ill-mannered mastiffs, big and dirty and doing exactly what they wanted.

"All right then, thank you for stopping by," Sonny said as she hugged her daughter.

"Give your grandmother a hug goodbye."

"No-no. Thank you, boys, I'm good. Next time, before you play by the creek."

Unfazed by anything the adults said, the boys climbed into the back of the Atlas.

"Mom, be careful. I want you to come back safe," Evanora said.

"I will, I promise. Don't worry about me, I'll be alright."

THE EARLY SPRING morning was still dark when she cranked up the truck and prepared to point it north. The dashboard read 32 degrees Fahrenheit, indicating there'd be a chance of snow. That's why she bought the two dry suits from Billy. One was packed away, while she planned on wearing the other today.

As the heat came on, a wave of Mitch's scent filled the truck, making a lump form in her throat. This time, she couldn't resist. Hot salty tears, seasoned by all the years, began to stream down her face. The chill of the morning lingered in the cab, but that wasn't what was making her cold. She had two options: spend the next half hour moving everything back to the Honda, holding a much higher risk of spilling everything across the road on a hard stop, or get used to the truck and all that it carried. Sonny didn't wipe away the tears. She wasn't wearing mascara. Tears had a way of drying on their own. She would have plenty of time to herself on the road ahead.

Sonny backed out of the driveway and shifted to first gear. She switched to second and picked up speed, finding herself on the interstate headed north. What the rest of the day had in store for her, she couldn't say. Mitch had explained to the girls, "A journey of a thousand miles begins with a single step, but so does an unpleasant journey, or a journey into darkness, or a journey through a difficult path, or a journey into the unknown. The first step is always the hardest, but it is never the last step." Today, she made that first step.

2

———

Sonny loved driving. She had taught Mitch to drive manual, and he had immediately taken to it like a horse to an open field. They had made it a point to teach their daughters how to drive a stick. On Saturdays, they always listened to the "Car Talk" radio program for mechanical awareness. "I'll take that with pride," she said to the spirit world. "No major accidents, and our vehicles have always been well-cared for." The little wins add up.

In Michigan, the farther one traveled north, the further one traveled back in time. The sun rose at 7:34 AM that day. Sonny enjoyed the pink and orange glow on her right. It marked the start of the sun's race across Lake Huron. As the sun peeked over the horizon, she crossed the Zilwaukee Bridge—a functional bridge that felt more like a rollercoaster with its dips and rises at 120 feet in the air. Each time she drove over it, she wondered if it might collapse, and if it would be better to take the long route around Saginaw. As a teen, "America," a song released by Simon & Garfunkel, mentioned it took four days to hitchhike from Saginaw to Pittsburgh. Saginaw "seemed like a dream." The Zilwaukee Bridge was a nightmare. The bridge had a reputation for being a fiasco: behind schedule, over budget, and loaded with fractures in need of repair. Unmarked landfills discovered during the construction of the ramps caused environmental damage. When Sonny was a little girl, she remembered a four-lane drawbridge that opened and closed for ships docking in Saginaw. Her father would let her out onto the stopped freeway to watch the ships pass from the railing. A great relief from sunny hours in the back seat of their Chevy. About the same time as that song came out.

Ten minutes past the bridge, Sonny decided to stop at the rest area before Pinconning. In summer, it would be bustling with people, cars, and dog walkers, all heading north to their cabins. But on that morning, it was only her and three semi-trucks letting their engines run at idle. Although Michigan was a four-season state, the early springtime seemed the loneliest. Before the snow melted or the blossoms and berries bloomed, everything looked murky. That first light and color starting her day were gone.

Sonny lumbered back to the truck, an image of Mitch and his half-cocked dream of penning a novel worming into her thoughts. This wouldn't be any ordinary piece of literature; it would scrutinize and appraise every last rest area lining the concrete veins of I-75. A whimsical concept let out with a sly chuckle; that was pure Mitch. He had joked, "Pure Mitch-igan" as a play on the state's television ads.

Half a decade back, Mitch had come barging into the parlor like a gust of wind. She was sitting, lost in the rhythmic dance of needle and thread, when he blurted out, "They've got a website up and running!"

"What website? Who on Earth are 'they'?" she queried, threading her needle through the eye of her confusion.

"Rest Area Ratings," he'd spat out before storming off in a huff. The whole time, he had been drumming up ideas in the quiet theater of his mind. Mitch always had plans.

It was a quick release of his frustration, but she knew. She knew most everything about Mitch. Given the time and opportunity, he would have traversed the north-and-south-bound interstate from Sault Ste. Marie, Ontario, to Miami, Florida, stopping and rating every rest area along the way.

"Would you have brought me with you?" Sonny asked out loud. "Or was this going to be one of your adventures? You know, you thought of it before Google, before the internet."

Sonny sat for a moment, enjoying the comfort of the leather seat warmer. The Honda was too old for these luxury features. It still had an ashtray. Mitch was full of good ideas. She admired that about him but wished he would have acted on them more often; would have taken action.

AT THE LAST exit before the Mackinac Bridge, Sonny stopped for lunch at Audie's. It had been there for as long as she could remember, or at least the building had. It was where they would always stop to eat. Not much had changed since she was a little girl. She could still remember when they added the salad bar in the '80s. The counter where the register sat now had a card reader where there used to be a sign reading "cash and travelers checks only."

She scanned the menu, recalling Mitch's go-to open-faced sandwich and his jabs at her predictable whitefish order. Glinda and Evanora were more fickle with their choices. "I'll have the open-faced turkey sandwich, Teresa. Thank you," she requested.

When the piping hot dish arrived, Sonny felt a lump form in her throat. She blotted away a tear with the napkin. The turkey was moist and flavored, bathed in savory gravy and accompanied by real, creamy mashed potatoes. This was no prefab fare assembled from a warehouse delivery. Someone had crafted this meal in the kitchen. As she savored the tangy cranberry sauce, Sonny went back to her childhood dinners at her grandmother's Detroit home. The brick house, once her mother's childhood home, teemed with relatives every weekend. Wedged between her boisterous aunt and uncle, she jostled for space at the table, piled high with hearty fare.

"I get why you loved this sandwich," Sonny murmured to the spirits.

After inspecting the canoe and its straps in the truck bed, she hopped back in the cab. The radio played the Mackinac Bridge Authority station's historical spiel. On loop, it recounted the impossible feat of constructing the "Bridge That Couldn't Be Built." Sonny knew this bridge well. On Labor Day weekends, her family joined thousands of others in a pilgrimage across the strait, traversing the five-mile span on foot. Breaking from tradition in later trips, they bypassed the bus lines and walked the bridge from north to south. Next, they ferried to Mackinac Island for a quick jaunt before returning to the car. By day's end, the southbound traffic had thinned, and they returned home faster. It was always a fun day with the girls.

On the north side of the bridge stood Castle Rock, a jagged pinnacle that afforded a breathtaking view of the peninsula. Photo albums brimmed with snapshots of the girls posing in front of the Paul Bunyan and Babe statues. Then they went up 171 steps to the top of Castle Rock. Cowering atop the rock, which seemed to sway with the slightest breeze hundreds of feet above the interstate, photos captured the fear on each face.

M-123 was a winding two-lane asphalt road snaking through the vast Hiawatha National Forest. Spanning roughly 900,000 acres of pine and birch woods planted during the Great Depression, it made a great drive. This forest was on the cusp of its hundredth anniversary. "Every visit north felt like a trip back in time," mused Sonny.

"That pack is bigger than you," said a man in the hotel parking lot.

Sonny balanced herself with the red dry-bag on her back and tightened the shoulder straps. "Thanks, I'm good," she replied with a smile and small wave, making her way toward the hotel lobby. She had parked her Tundra next to a life-sized illuminated moose statue. She thought the light would deter anyone from tampering with the lock on her Prospector and mountain bike.

"We don't have a restaurant here, but there's a McDonald's across the road. They have the best internet in town," the front desk clerk informed her as she checked in.

With the key in hand, Sonny climbed up the stairs to the second floor. Each step felt heavier with the weight of her pack, but the room was clean and comfortable. Fast food wasn't her first choice, so she left her pack in the room and drove into town to explore other options.

Driving north off the parking lot, Sonny could see why the hotel desk called it "the valley." The road led down to the Tahquamenon River Valley, with miles of wilderness. Her dinner at the "family bar" on Railroad Street was slow to arrive but filling, causing her stomach to gurgle throughout the night. She woke and looked out the window twice during the night to check on the life-sized moose. It was doing its job watching over the truck.

The next morning, Sonny was the first in the breakfast nook. Her natural inclination was to help the woman set up coffee and eggs. Afterward, she put on her pack and climbed back into the Tundra. It was still dark as she headed north on M-123 toward a "road" labeled 500. The pavement ended when she turned and she knew in an instant that taking the Tundra had been the right choice. Sand, snow, and frozen mud welcomed her on the twisted trail. She followed the tracks from the previous explorer to avoid getting stuck and shifted into high four-wheel drive. The satellite radio lost connection eight times during the next thirty minutes.

As the road curved left, Sonny's attention went to a giant pool of muddy ice that covered a third of the road. Tire tracks had gone through the center, leaving it cracked like an icy broken shell of crème brûlée.

With a sudden, abrupt stop, Sonny mashed the brakes. Numerous items burst forth from under the passenger seat, scattering haphazardly. An imposing figure locked gazes with her, half-standing in the dusty road ahead. A formidable black bear was before her, with brawny legs and enormous paws. Its wide head was adorned with two rounded ears, akin to satellite dishes. The bear halted, its warm breath fading into the cool air. Nose lifted, it scrutinized the colossal machine Sonny was commanding. Curiosity ensnared the majestic beast.

As it sniffed at the vehicle's hood, the bear reared up on its muscular hind legs, front paws examining the company emblem affixed to the front. Under the beast's weight, the metal began to warp. It ascended further, striving to meet Sonny's gaze. A deep, resonant snort and a flick of its snout, merely feet away from the windshield, sent a wave of goose-bumps cascading down her arms and spine. Razor-sharp claws grazed the sleek paint, marring the surface. The claw tips burrowed into the hood for better leverage. In response, Sonny hammered on the horn with all her might. Startled and now aware that this wasn't a meal but a frightening, noisy contraption, the bear thumped back down to the ground. The beast's paws were strong enough to bear its 400-pound weight and burrow through a beaver lodge. It gathered momentum, surging over a small mound, and melted away into the forest, soundlessly. The magnificent creature assimilated into the woodland's backdrop, vanishing from sight. Her heart hammered against her chest, serving as a potent reminder of the perils that lay ahead. Fear caused Sonny's forehead to glisten.

"So, that's a bear," she breathed out, her whisper barely audible. Her right foot eased off the brake while her left pressed down on the clutch, adrenaline coursing through her leg muscles. The truck lurched forward in first gear, inching about a hundred yards before she gingerly applied the brake and shifted into park.

In the footwell lay the bounty of her discovery, revealed by momentum. A metal box, an empty Faygo bottle, a clean pair of white underwear, and a tee shirt belonging to Mitch.

Sonny picked up the box, surprised by its weight. With a click, she opened it to reveal the handgun Mitch had denied having, its clip full and secure in formed foam. Checking the chamber, she found a single round. Etched into the metal were the words "Glock 21 gen4 USA .45 Auto."

Returning everything to its place, Sonny muttered to the spirits, "We both had secrets." She took a deep breath and shifted the truck into gear, catching a whiff of Mitch's scent. She could sense him everywhere, haunting her like a ghost. But she had to be brave and push through the memories, for the task at hand awaited her.

The sign for Two-Hearted River State Forest Campground brought a sense of relief. Sonny wasn't lost. She could do this. But as she turned onto the "road" marked 423, she muttered to the spirits, "'Campground' is being generous. They should include 'Rustic' in the description." This was the kind of place Mitch would have loved. A suspended wooden bridge crossed the river north to the dunes of Lake Superior. A hand-painted sign next to one of the two buildings read "Two-Hearted Chapel." But Sonny focused on the task at hand.

THE SUN HIGHER. The air crisp. The grass slick underfoot. Sonny unlocked her bike and canoe. She lifted the mountain bike from the bed of the truck with care. Next, she found a trustworthy-looking tree off the path and locked it with a chain. It seemed hidden.

Driving to the drop-off, she noted key markers along the way: the tree full of hand-painted directional signs, a giant painted lumber mill saw blade, and the state Chris Brown Lake sign.

There was an inconceivable giant rock. It reminded her of one of her favorite movies, *The Princess Bride*, where "inconceivable" brought the classic quote, "I don't think that word means what you think it means." This she would remember as the Princess Bride Rock.

Finally, Sonny reached 407, the Pine Stump Junction—the blacktop leading to her drop point on the High Bridge. The truck made this trip easy. What waited for her around that next turn?

The High Bridge was once the crossing point. After the center pylon washed out sometime in the 1930s, the two remaining stone pylons remained. A group of men from the CCC cut a new road—the one she drove in on. These two tracks for the original bridge remained secluded. The good people of the north wouldn't bother the truck parked here while she dropped her canoe. It should be fine here for the week.

Standing on the concrete pylon's edge, the Two-Hearted looked fast. Sonny wondered if she was up for the river, as the river was up. She walked back to the truck, parked further off to the roadside, and removed the Prospector from the bed. Unleashed from the straps, it was easy to lift over her head. She navigated the loose rocks on the slope with care. The Prospector down on safe ground, she went back up the steep incline of the bank.

In the rear cab seat was her red dry-bag backpack. After retrieving this, a trip down to the canoe. One last trip and she removed the 30-gallon blue barrel with backpack-like straps. With this, she locked the truck. Sonny laughed when the alarm chirped, knowing only the bear would care.

A finger in the water and she was glad Billy had talked her into the taupe-colored dry suit. The putty color might hide some of the dirt and muck she was sure to fall in. The blue barrel found its spot in the front of the Prospector and the red dry-bag was placed behind her seat.

Getting into a canoe was hard and made one look ridiculous. Mitch would say, "You look like a monkey fucking a football." One last check of her life jacket, ball cap on, Sonny picked up her primary paddle and gave a push on the canoe. It didn't move. So, Sonny made a second attempt. It moved.

Friction stopped working against her once the Prospector got to the wet, soft bank. The nose dipped in and moved under her control with ease. The edge of the blade pushed deep into the mud bank. The nose pointed downstream, slipping into the cool waters, breaking the surface with the slightest *swish*. The real adventure was starting.

The water took over, causing a sway in her balance. Instinctively, she leaned the other way, fighting against the water's force. Her mistake was overcompensating; her weight was multiplied by all the gear.

Time slowed down during pivotal moments in life. Plunging into an icy river, one could reflect on many things. Some were regrets, such as, "Was this a good idea?" Others were more trivial, like, "This rubber suit is hot, but the cold water is refreshing." Significant memories stayed with you forever, such as the birth of a child or meeting a true love. Yet, at this moment, her thought was simple: "I should have bought a helmet."

3

Everything stayed with the Prospector. It had been a good and loyal friend, as promised, the tie-straps proving their worth. After dumping out the water, Sonny found herself a yard downstream from where she had started. The blue ball cap she had worn on her neighborhood walks was now lost to the river. She hoped that some desperate camper might find it on a hot day when they needed it most.

Sonny reached into her dry-bag and pulled out a large-billed garden hat with a drawstring. It was squishy enough to fit into anything and would float if she capsized again. She knew there was no fooling herself; this would happen again. After inspecting the sore spot on her head, she confirmed that it was only a bruise with no broken skin.

With the canoe back in the water, Sonny did a quick

check of her emergency gear before pushing off. Her hands frisked her torso. She felt the emergency knife strapped to her chest. The bear horn dangled on the clip. A bulge in her chest pocket, the orange satellite emergency beacon. Finally, the torso zipper pocket with her flint striker kit. All boxes checked. She dipped her paddle in the water and used the forward stroke to push off. This was followed by a J-stroke to gain momentum, slipping into the water's current. Within minutes, she had covered a significant distance. Much better than her last attempt. Her confidence grew as she began to gain control over the canoe.

Heading down the Two-Hearted River, Sonny appreciated the silence. She hadn't experienced this kind of quiet in a long time. The only sounds were the gentle lapping of the river and the noises of the north woods. No phone, no kids, no one asking for a sandwich or arguing with their sister. It was only Sonny and the river, her only friend the Prospector 14. The only thing that mattered was staying upright and dry, avoiding rocks and logs. Yes—physically demanding, it made it much simpler to focus on the moment at hand.

She could see the appeal her daughter's generation found in the age of modern expedition. Converting a van to live campsite to campsite while working remotely had a sense of romance. It was very American to want freedom and independence. It was less expensive than paying rent or utility bills. When your backyard is the National Parks or wooded beauty of the north, it's hard to consider anything else. She had seen videos posted on YouTube from through-hikers, van builders, and global sailors. Built on these experiences, there was always a boy or girl looking into the phone's camera, saying, "I will never be the same." Smiles from sunburned faces who traversed thousands of miles declaring that something had transformed them to their souls.

Its seed germinated in the late nineties with Bill Bryson's *A Walk in the Woods: Rediscovering America.* Mitch had read it first. She had a pile of other books to read on her nightstand before that one. Its movie adaptation was more consumable, and who doesn't like Robert Redford?

Sonny approached a fallen red pine in the river. Its roots displaced a massive volume of earth on the bank that looked to Sonny like a half-opened can lid. The tree trunk lay half in the river, with branches jutting out in every direction. Sonny had to decide whether to try to make it over the trunk or to portage around through the muck and mud. She slowed the canoe, steadying the paddle, until the bow tapped the fallen tree. Her free hand snaked into her backpack and she retrieved the folding saw with its two-foot blade. Billy had been right; she needed it.

She secured the canoe alongside the tree. Sonny unfolded the blade and began clearing out the smaller branches. The green, gooey cuts told her that these branches were not suitable to save for the fire. She would need to find dry wood later on. With the branches cleared, Sonny worked the paddle to push the bow over the lowest section of the trunk. Next, she began to scoot the hull over the protrusion. When the Prospector 14 was solid in place a third of the way, Sonny stepped out onto the massive trunk of the red pine. She bent over to pull the canoe over the rest of the way. Life was now a delicate balance of brute force and grace. Her goal was to get over and move on. With a firm hand on the grip and shaft of her paddle, Sonny pushed off stern-first and floated down the river. Three well-timed draw strokes later, she was straight and true again. The tranquility of the lapping water and ripples in the Two-Hearted River gave her a sense of peace. This was why she had come to the river—to prove to herself that she could do something difficult and demanding.

Happiness shattered. She rounded the bend, a great red maple sprawled across the water, its bulk linking bank to river. Part of it bobbed in the current's embrace. Slowing her Prospector, she assessed the scene, eyeing the left bank where the tree bridged the river. A path lay beneath, requiring branch removal, fraught with danger—a falling giant could crush her. She paddled right, circling, contemplating her path. The trunk was wedged in mud, supported by the bank, and branches skimmed the water's surface, hinting at a passable route.

Again the saw blade moved back and forth, creating a mound of sawdust mixing with water in the boat's bottom. Sonny felt sore, unlike anything she had felt at home loading the dishwasher, gardening, taking walks, riding bikes, or moving Mitch's bedding. The burn concentrated in her shoulder and arms. She finished cutting the last of the larger branches and spotted a safe passage. The low centerline seat in the Prospector made it easier to lean back and go under the trunk.

She stored the saw away. Sonny took a few strong strokes and turned, attempting to align the canoe with the river. She allowed the water to carry her and adjusted her paddle and lean, almost succeeding.

The sound of a canoe's hull hitting the rough bark of a Michigan red maple was distinctive. The uneven, harsh, and grating sound of the Kevlar and gel coating against the tree's bark sounded worse than nails on a chalkboard. Its sound nullified any manufacturer guarantee in seconds. The rasping and intermittent high-pitched squeaks from the friction points along the canoe's skin, scraping against the unseen branches under the icy waters, sent chills up her spine. As she leaned back as far as her spine would allow, dead leaves rustled in her ears. The water lapped and rippled against the boat's sides, and her body shifted to see the progress she had made, causing the trunk to creak under the weight shift. A flop sweat broke out across her brow when she thought the tree was falling. Without warning, all the sounds and fury stopped, leaving only the water and breeze. She made it through. She would try to portage next time.

An hour before sunset, as darkness descended, Sonny needed to find a spot to camp for the night. Her progress was not as fast as she had anticipated. Looking at the map Billy sold her, she realized she was still a distance from the first campground. She needed a flat spot for her tent, or the right pair of trees for her hammock, and she needed a high landing from the waterline. Her day had been about taking time to get things right. Now, with the day ending, it was a race against the setting sun to find a dry and safe place. But where?

4

Sonny could see the river continuing on through the trees. She cut the water with her paddle and turned toward the sandy bank of the river's peninsula. Her momentum carried her forward. She stood and balanced, then stepped out of the Prospector 14 into the shallow water. Gripping the bow handle with both hands, she lifted and leaned back with all her weight, heaving the canoe forward. With a second lurch, she landed. One of her kits included a rope and four small steel pulleys, each the size of a credit card and rated for 500 lbs. Sonny lashed the red nylon cord and two of the pulleys to the handle, sending the other end to a sturdy tree on the river's edge. Pulleys eased her work, locking her progress after each pull; the canoe inched up the sandy bank.

Sonny was warm and removed a layer to avoid sweating.

Staying dry was important. This was one of the lessons from scouts that stayed fresh with her all these years. Get hot and perspire. Perspiration freezes, body temperature drops, and you get hypothermia. Taking off layers and adjusting is better.

She walked a few steps into the woods to find a fire ring and stone seating. Someone had made a nice resting space.

Setting up camp was Sonny's first priority. She decided to use the hammock sleeping system instead of a tent on the ground. Her first attempt at setting it up seemed off. Ten more minutes, the sun almost gone, it was close enough. Dry fallen branches and sticks were the next priority. Nothing bigger than her wrist, she remembered from her scouts camp, and she gathered what she could. Darkness had arrived. Her last few pieces were picked and cut from a dead white birch; the paper-like bark would make ideal kindling.

Hungry, tired, and the cold creeping in, Sonny put on her camp outfit. She hung the dry suit, socks, and pants inside out on the hammock line to dry. Sonny had lost the daily race with the sun and worked by the light of her headlamp. The hatchet from her kit split the sticks into small burnable pieces. The little mound of twigs that looked like a bird's nest sat there cold. She struck the flint stick again, making quick and short sparks, but nothing hot or lasting for the fire. Her motivation waning, she started to rub it in frustration rather than swipe it one stroke at a time. A cascade of sparks and light like July fireworks landed on the pile, igniting the nest. Huh? That's how it works. Her desperation subsided.

The freeze-dried pack of food came out of her kit, along with the tiny simple stove and cooking pot. Did she need the titanium utensils? No. But they worked great and saved weight. Once the water boiled, it went into the pack and was sealed. She would never tell anyone about the burn from touching the pot without a rag or the spill of boiling water on her leg. Three times the amount she would eat at any one normal meal, the Mountain Swedish Meatballs were salty and filling. She ate so fast, it felt like a rock sitting in her belly when she was finished.

The stone seating warmed from the fire. She thought to herself, *Whoever made this seating knew what they were doing.* She was off the ground and comfortable. Sonny watched the flames of the fire dance, feeling a sense of accomplishment from her day.

Sonny wanted to be like those fresh faces from the young generation on video exploring the world. She wanted to have a great adventure and see the world. That would take a lot more energy than what she had. So far, reality only made her feel every mile driven, each stroke paddled, and a sense of being wet and cold. That moment, the feeling of "I'll never be the same" still evaded her. Was it at the end of the river?

CLICK. A sound in the distance sent her heart racing. She looked in the direction of the sound. On her feet and back to the safety of the canoe, she clutched the bear horn tight. Her eyes searching the darkness, she walked backward to the stone seat and fire pit. *CLICK.*

Still, there was nothing and no one. "Paranoid? Or feeling guilty?" she said out loud. As she waited for something—anything—everything began to slow, and her adrenaline lowered. She sat on the warm stone seat, vigilant, watching into the dark woods.

Full belly, weary from the day's toil, she unzipped the hammock cover and settled, leaning back. For the first time, she raised her gaze. Stars adorned the sky. The entire Milky Way painted the night sky with dots reminiscent of Pollock's art. This was the reason for her journey. The beauty of the north woods defied her meager vocabulary. The air, pure and cool, offered rejuvenation.

"I know I am never alone," she uttered to the spirits. "There must be something more."

DAYLIGHT GREETED HER. It was the longest stretch of slumber she had experienced since Mitch's passing. The fresh air filled her lungs, and she cherished the moment.

CLICK. Something in the woods startled her. "Guilty," she said. It was time to move once more.

Clean, pack, filter water, change into the dry suit and gear. Reaching into the blue barrel, she retrieved several snack bars. She had neglected to do this the previous day, unable to find the opportune moment on the river. The crack in the plastic wrapper and unveiling of chocolate granola brought immense satisfaction. Quick and available energy had the potential to become addictive. Her body sought easy calories. But she limited herself to one bar for breakfast, reserving the rest for her day.

Grit coated the hull as the canoe glided into the Two-Hearted. A frosty mist hovered above the water, mimicking fog. She drifted through the haze with a sense of icy touch on her skin—almost like snowflakes, but in a gentle mist.

The Two-Hearted resembled the color of root beer. Rivers and waterfalls in this region owed their hue to the tannic acids borne by the cedar swamps. When little, the girls believed the nearby Tahquamenon River was made of root beer. In summer, the churning waters over the falls frothed and foamed, resembling the head on a glass of beer. Mitch suggested the girls bend down and take a sip. The two learned fast, valuable lessons. First, the Tahquamenon River was not a creation of Roald Dahl's Wonka Chocolate Factory. Second, their father possessed a brand of humor that aimed to teach them to think.

Sonny had always admired that aspect of Mitch. He challenged her to be less gullible, making it difficult for others to take advantage of her. When they first met, she found this quality attractive. Mitch was not one to agree to her every command. Some of the boys she dated perceived her physical allure as a form of mind control. They lost their ability to think for themselves, instead behaving like loyal dogs rather than men vying for her affections. All that seemed like a lifetime ago. She didn't even encounter Mitch until she was twenty-eight. The twins arrived two years later. Now, standing on the far side of the actuarial table contemplating a future without Mitch filled her with uncertainty. It frightened her more than unfamiliar noises in the nocturnal woods.

The early sun's golden glow, dissolving the frozen mist, appeared enchanting. Two sandhill cranes, reminiscent of prehistoric creatures, stood on the riverbank, both adorned in crimson plumage. With a resounding honk and bugle, they seemed to convey, "Stay away, for this is my domain." Sonny had harbored a constant hope of sighting a common loon during her visits to the northern woods. The haunting, memorable cry of the bird in the morning ranked among her favorite sounds. Loons suffered from the cruelty of evolution. They needed water. With feet set far to the rear of their body, taking flight required vast lakes and open bodies of water. The Two-Hearted lacked the runway required for loons to land and take flight. Loons liked flat and glassy waters. The Two-Hearted churned and remained rapid between its banks. Nonetheless, there remained a glimmer of hope, as their calls could sound miles away. Tonight?

SONNY MISTOOK it for a beaver dam. Beavers were well known to obstruct waterways and flood swamps, less likely on fast-flowing rivers like this one. As she drew near, the true nature of the obstacle became plain: a logjam. A colossal jack pine, too massive to perch on the sandy banks, had fallen across the river. Last season, she might have maneuvered beneath it. But this year, the larger limbs and driftwood had taken up residence in the shelter of the fallen pine.

Extending her blade, Sonny steered the canoe toward the shore, embedding the bow in the soft bank with a resounding slurp in the muck. It would have been a flawless landing if she were a pilot. Keeping her balance with the paddle, she made her way to the front of the canoe. Stepping onto the shore and tugging at the handle, she inched the Prospector higher up.

"Some folks prefer the bungee strap," she recalled Billy's advice. "I find the paracord tie to be more to my liking." Billy explained that the degradation of the material paracord was slower. It provided a stronger hold when tied right. Now, she needed to remember how to tie knots.

Her paddle and reserve secured to the thwart that spanned the two outer edges. These edges were gunwales, protruding outward to maintain rigidity. The removable and adjustable yoke rested on the centerline for her to carry. Billy had taught her a trick. Instead of having to adjust the yoke each time, they had measured it once in the store and marked the center with nautical tape. The yoke positioned on one gunwale, she could apply pressure to the opposite side—less than half an inch—and the yoke would snap into place.

Leveraging her leg muscles, Sonny hoisted the blue barrel on her back and embarked on the first trip. She traversed the towpath. She climbed the sandy ridge. Pine needles blanketed the forest floor. She was very careful to avoid the interlaced roots. It was a weighty load, but she could manage. Her bear horn at the ready, she remained vigilant, scanning her surroundings.

"Slow and steady wins this race, Mitch," she whispered to the realm of spirits.

When the river appeared clear, she followed the path to the water's edge, intending to lower the barrel. But, upon arrival, she spotted another logjam fifty yards downstream. The proximity of the two obstructions seemed illogical. It would be more practical to traverse and portage such a short stretch.

"Howdy," a male voice called out.

Startled by the unexpected greeting, an involuntary release of pee occurred. Her hand instinctively reached for the bear horn, and she let out a brief blast. It wasn't until she realized the intruder was a man that her vise-like grip on the horn relaxed.

"Whoa. Whoa," he exclaimed, placing his free hand over his ear. "Didn't mean to startle you, ma'am." With his palm

facing forward, he displayed a gesture of calm and friendship. His other hand gripped a chainsaw.

"Dear Lord," Sonny exclaimed.

"Bit jumpy? First time out here?" he inquired.

"How did you know?"

"Your equipment is still clean and in one piece. Must be
her maiden voyage."

"First trip."

"Don't mind me. My place is a mile that way," he said,
nodding to the right. "I cleared a path on the tree up there
yesterday, but ran out of fuel. Thought I'd come back and
tackle this one."

Sonny nodded. "Wow," she replied, still buzzing with
adrenaline. "That's great. Thank you."

The two gazed at each other, unsure, looking.

"Well, why don't we switch? I need to get out there for the
branches, and you need to retrieve your gear."

"Good idea." She stepped up and forward while he
descended past her toward the tree. A scent of gasoline, oil,
fresh cut wood, and the musky odor of an unwashed man
filled the air. These aromas transported her back to last
summer when Mitch mowed the lawn, trimmed the hedges,
and worked alongside her in the garden. She hadn't realized
how much she longed for that fragrance again. It possessed a
potent allure.

Sonny placed the blue barrel by a large tree off the path.

The small engine chugged with the first pull of the rope. On the second attempt, the chainsaw roared to life. Knowing there was another person nearby put her at ease. The noise would deter bears. The return trips with her dry-bag and the Prospector were quicker than the first. She could hear the man sawing through the branches. The high revs were a signal of the destruction of wooden fibers. On her third trip, she found the perfect balance with the yoke. The canoe felt lighter than the previous two journeys but remained unwieldy. Overhanging branches proved difficult to pass. Roots on the path seemed to reach out like "hand-mines," grabbing at her toes, entangling her feet in an attempt to enforce the penalties of gravity. Gravity always wins in the end. The ornery trees were no different from the apple trees Dorothy faced in Oz.

The sound of sawing ceased by the time she reached the water's edge with the canoe, the barrel, and pack fastened. With her paddle in hand, untied and at the ready, she heard the man call out, "That's a mighty fine boat you have there."

"Thank you."

"Stick to the far bank on the left. You should navigate past that tree. You can't see it from here, but it's a clear passage."

"Thank you. Thank you for clearing the trees."

"You take care now."

Sonny felt a sense of unease and impoliteness for not inquiring about his name or offering her own. His gray hair and beard, along with his calm demeanor, suggested he was a decent man. Still, she had to focus on her own interests here. Engaging in a conversation with a stranger would cost her time. Although pleasant, it would steal time from the remaining daylight.

"Thanks! You too. It's going to be a great day." She pushed off, floating a few feet, sliding into her seat, and began to paddle.

"Stay to your left, on the left," he called out.

She started to discern the opening he had described, and lifting her paddle, she called back, "Thank you, I see it."

He was right. It was clear and safe. "Should I have befriended that man? Would that have been part of my transformation from exploration?" she asked Mitch, who never answered.

5

There was a happy dream Sonny wished for each night. Finding the rustic campground and depositing five dollars in the dropbox, she ate dinner after setting up camp. Swinging in the hammock and looking up to the galaxy, she hoped to dream that dream again.

Engulfed by a blend of hope and unease, Sonny found herself navigating a surreal landscape. The hope stemmed from the emotions evoked by this enigmatic dream, yet the fear that it might be her last loomed. As if from a distant, celestial realm, Sonny found herself returning home—a place both comforting and familiar.

Here, beloved aunts and uncles, childhood friends, and neighborhood acquaintances beckoned her, eager to share the transformations that had unfolded since her last sojourn.

The discontinued Faygo Rock & Rye pop she adored in childhood filled the garage fridge, the scent of her mother's signature meatball dish wafted from the kitchen, and her father, pipe in hand, perused the newspaper in the living room, peeking over its edge to offer a warm smile and wink. A palpable sense of love and security permeated the air, promising a solace that felt real.

This sanctuary existed just around the corner, at the next bend, or behind a door, if only she could unlock it. Immersed in an intricate web of love, a potent spiritual energy enveloped her, guiding her onward. Upon awakening, the lingering afterglow from this ethereal visit suffused her life for weeks.

It had been ages since Sonny last experienced this dream, or even one similar. It had graced her slumber only three times in her life, a potent force that consumed her. She guarded it at arm's length. It echoed the descriptions found in near-death experiences. She couldn't help but ponder if death enticed the living toward a final light, flooding their senses with intoxication.

As more friends and family took up residence in this transcendent realm, their voices swelled into a chorus, calling to Sonny like the sirens of myth.

CLICK. Waking from the noise, Sonny told herself that it's the woods. Nothing had followed her this distance to eat her or attack. She was safe, cocooned in the warmth of her hammock. Billy had sold her the whole system, which included the extra padding, wind screen, mosquito net, rain flap, and cover. In one moment, she knew she was a hanging human Twinkie waiting for some bear to discover her and treat her like a piñata. In the next, she was off the ground and hard to reach for most critters to care.

Her eyes opened a few minutes before the sunrise, at her circadian rhythm. She started to do the math in her head to answer the question, "What day is it?" A day of travel, half a day to start, camping on the river's peninsula, and then yesterday. She had taken two days to get to where she wanted to be after the first. Her muscles sore, joints stiff, she was going to need momentum to get out of the hammock. She needed the first movement to get going. "Oil can," she quoted the Tin Man.

Unzipping the one layer, she could feel the cold creep in. It motivated her to get moving. Her legs were fine; it was her arms and shoulder that were the problem. Once the dry suit was on, things started to warm up again. On the floor of the woods, soft pine needles cushioned her knees on the earth. She began to stretch and warm up. A salute to the sun, downward dog, hip flexor, and butterfly, and Sonny was ready for the rest of the day.

The water pot she had put on the fire before her stretch was now boiling. Breakfast included the cinnamon oatmeal packet with her banana. The simple hot meal filled her with warmth and energy.

Her blue barrel packed fast. The dry bag closed with a

click. The Prospector 14 rolled over with all the needles and overnight passengers evacuated. Snapping her life vest and checking her essentials, she looked downriver and thought, *This is going to be a good day.*

MINUTES DOWN THE RIVER, Sonny allowed her mind to time travel. They had decided to avoid any class reunions. People only got weirder with age. He didn't know anyone and played the supportive husband. She didn't know anyone in his class and played the dutiful wife. Decades later, those they did remember carried some unnecessary emotional baggage. He did this. She did that. One time they said that... It had always reminded her of a popular song by the Doobie Brothers when she was younger, "What a Fool Believes." That whole summer after it came out, she thought it was romantic and wonderful, being a fool for love. Reading the lyrics on the album changed that quickly. The "fool" was one of those boys she went to school with. Boys who always thought there was something more, when she hardly knew them, or remembered their names. At each reunion, they would come to her and explain something imagined between them. How they held a moment of silence the day she and Mitch married, knowing she was no longer available. Polite and patient, she would smile, nod, and give Mitch the signal. He always saved her from the awkward moments. She would miss that. Losing that one thing made her feel alone more than anything else in the world. It was something she might never be able to recover or recreate. Like a million little moments, there could never be anyone like Mitch.

All the drama helped Sonny appreciate what her girls were going through as they grew up. "Things were different back then" was a sentiment she often heard, but she didn't agree. Under the age of twenty, everything seemed heightened. Feelings, passions, ideas, growth spurts, changes, but that's just growing up.

It was the intensity that seemed amplified for the young girls. As a child, Sonny had perceived it as the result of peer pressure and the need to fit in with the right clique. For the twins, the judgments were harsh and unyielding—if a girl didn't eat, she was anorexic. Overweight? Labeled morbidly obese. If she had slept with a boy, branded a whore. If she had never kissed, a prude. It required adherence to the perfect beauty routine. They must dedicate more time and attention to attire. Her girls got subjected to a myriad of social pressures. Similar to her experience, but more intense for the twins.

Sonny remembered the first time she quoted her mother, "I am not your friend, I am your mother. My job is to make sure you're better than me."

It surprised Sonny. She understood it completely in an instant. Once the words left her lips, she knew her mother was right. She called her mother an hour later and thanked her.

"You're welcome."

"It's tough being a good mom. How did you do it?"

"You weren't as difficult as you think. You were more of a molehill girl than a mountain."

It brought a smile to her face to think about her mom. What would she think of this adventure? Her paddle stroke pushed her forward around the bend to face another chance for portage.

The Two-Hearted held many turns. It made the distance longer than the straighter rivers in the lower peninsula. It reminded her of one of those odd "fun facts" that Europe's coastline is 2-3 times longer than Africa's. Having fewer ports to support shipping kept Africa from being seafaring. Other parts of the world, with more natural ports, advanced to the waters, creating empires from navigable opportunities.

Having set down the blue barrel, she returned for the red dry-bag. That's when it happened—a hand-mine. Her ankle caught on a protruding root, sending her plummeting forward with no control. Instinctively, she stretched out her hands, hoping to save her teeth and avoid breaking her nose. Her hand reached out, and while falling, she heard the distant call of a loon echo, signaling the presence of a lake nearby.

Her eyes fluttered open, lashes sweeping dirt away. The metallic taste of iron from blood filled her mouth. Something had gotten cut or broken. Then, the familiar sensations of searing pain and electric jolts coursed through her nervous system to her brain. Her ankle, twisted and bruised, a consequence of her momentary lapse in attention. As for her wrist—was it sprained or broken? And what of her head —bruised or lacerated? She couldn't be certain. How long had she been out?

6

It was surprise. No, shock. Wait, or was this confusion? Sonny cried out in frustration, furious at her own negligence that had led to this predicament. A momentary lapse in attention. Stupid. She began to squirm, maneuvering her body until she lay on her back, her face liberated from the dirt. The once comforting, earthy scent of pine and soil had lost its charm.

Pain radiated from various points on her body—her head, ankle, arm. She felt fortunate. She had escaped a serious injury like a bruised rib or broken neck. Despite the pain, she considered herself lucky.

Sonny lay on her back on the trail, halfway between the blue barrel and the red dry-bag. Which one held the medical kit? She shut her eyes, imagining and playing the day back, recalling the morning's packing. Not long ago, she had been optimistic about the day ahead, self-congratulatory, boasting about the benefits of her stretching routine. Now, the second wave of pain was setting in, the type that lingers long after the adrenaline has worn off.

A flash of past experiences—standing at a bus stop in biting winter cold, the wind slicing through her jacket at eight years old. Two years later, the first day at a new school, standing on the playground looking down at her legs, noticing they were hairy, embarrassed and ashamed. An unsettling tumble from her bike, the embarrassment of being different. She had always told her girls to pick them-selves up; to push through the discomfort. "You are fine. Get back up."

She had to sit up. The movement was as simple as bending at the waist. She felt something warm trickle down her forehead. Bird droppings? Pine sap? Touching it, her fingers came away stained with blood.

The fleeting embarrassment subsided. She began to think. The blue barrel held the ropes and pulleys that could aid her mobility. It also contained food and water to sustain her. The red dry-bag held the emergency beacon and cell phone. If she could reach halfway, she could go all the way. The plan remained the same: red dry-bag first, then the blue barrel, then the Prospector.

She examined her wrist—was it broken or sprained? She pulled back the sleeve of her dry suit. Her fingers still moved —good. The bone was straight—good. The wrist was tender and turning purple. Her left foot throbbed with pain at the slightest movement.

"Here goes," she whispered to the wilderness. Sonny flipped over onto her stomach. With her elbows bent to protect her hands and wrist, she nudged herself forward. Right knee, push, move forward, shift hip, left knee, push, move forward. "A hundred more like that."

At this level, she noticed an early season mushroom. It was a detail she missed on the first trip and would have missed in each passing. To distract herself from the pain, she told herself a story. She thought about the Northwoods Giant Fungus from Michigan. A fungus the size of a blue whale, one single organism that was 2,500 years old and spanned 180 acres of Michigan forest. What was it called? The Armadillo? How was she going to remember it? Jerry Garcia? The Armillaria gallica. This story spilled over to another. The ant "supercolonies" that divided North America. Entire states of ants working together, unified in efforts, clashing with rival factions. And the poor fool in the story who built a house on the front line of the two fighting factions. He lost it all. She needed to be an ant.

Almost there. I can make it.

7

A bit further. One more nudge, two. "I have this within me," Sonny reassured herself. She hauled herself up the side of the Prospector 14. The red dry-bag, she remembered—hope. Using all her strength, she tipped the canoe on its side until it disgorged the red dry-bag onto her. She rolled aside, allowing the bag to rest on the ground. Within a few clicks, it opened and spread out. Her arm reached inside, feeling the useful items she craved to access. With a sigh, she faced the harsh truth. The medical kit was in the blue barrel.

The palm-sized orange satellite emergency beacon was in the red dry-bag. Hope. She had removed it from her dry suit's zipped pocket the day before to make room for more energy bars. *I am going to be okay.* She turned the beacon on by pressing the power for two seconds. She could see the simple black-and-white display come on. It buffered. A yellow light turned on. Its bars indicated full power. Each letter scrolled across the little low-definition screen. The message said "Welcome." *I am going to make it. Things will be fine. Stay calm.* "Please call our service number or visit our website to subscribe."

"What? WHAT? WHAT THE FUCK? You have to subscribe for service!" Her vulgarity echoed across the waters, sending two mallards to flight in fear.

Pain brought her priorities back in order. The yelp had strained something, creating a sharp headache. She ripped her pristine white cotton underwear, reserved for the journey home. One half—the elastic band and cotton prepped to fasten over her head. First, she plucked the foil hand sanitizer packets from a side pocket. Holding a small travel mirror, she put on a brave face before confronting her reflection. The face staring back was unfamiliar. She wished she had spared herself the sight. Using the "clean" water from her drinking bottle, she dampened a sports bra, also reserved for the trip home. She dabbed at the dried blood on her forehead. She cleaned her face as best she could. *How did I hit my head in the same place twice on one trip?* She opened a foil hand sanitizer packet and cleaned her hands. Another foil packet opened, and she braced for the inevitable sting. The pain forced her breath into short, sharp gasps, pained moans escaping her lips. But it still didn't measure up to childbirth. The clean underwear, fastened tight around her head, provided pressure. It would shield her from most dirt during her return trip.

"Ugh," she vocalized her frustration. "How am I going to manage this, Mitch? I'm not sure I can make two trips, and I doubt I can haul it all in one."

The sun had retreated behind the clouds, bringing a chill to the air. The wind picked up. Sonny retrieved the map from inside the canoe.

The scooching technique proved least painful and most effective. Submerged in the chilly river, the flow of water around her legs provided a soothing massage. The temperature in her dry suit began to drop. The coolness offered relief to her injured ankle. She toyed with the idea of slicing off the dry suit leg to let the cold take over. Her emergency blade snapped back into place on her chest when she decided against it. She knew that indecision could be perilous. This only made her question each choice more.

Splashing about in the water like an overgrown child, Sonny began to assess her situation. She tried to muster clarity and focus. A paddle could serve as a crutch or a splint. A stick could also be a splint. Her folding saw, a green sapling the diameter of her thumb, could be cut for the splint. Stripping the bark in long cuts, she could weave fresh bark into a makeshift rope.

Returning to the Prospector 14, she extracted her reliable folding saw. Next, she scooted back into the woods where she found two saplings about the right size. After a few minutes of sawing, both trees fell, and she returned to the comforting muck of the river. Her injured leg went back in the water. The distraction of activity kept her mind off her wrist, though there was an occasional reminder that flashed, urging her to handle it with care.

With steady hands, she cut a quarter-inch wide line along each sapling. Once her pile of strips was complete, she took four slices and began a simple weave. This was like her friendship bracelets at camp. After about thirty minutes, she had created several feet of sturdy twine.

Next, Sonny's attention turned to the splints. Using the saw, she transformed the two stripped saplings into four equal lengths. She fixed them tight, not taut, to avoid cutting off circulation. She flexed again. Her stretching was not the usual morning routine. Instead, it was an effort in strapping the four matched pieces to her leg above and below the ankle under the icy water. Her final binding secured below the knee.

With the task accomplished, she felt a sudden decline in everything. Her energy, adrenaline, and motivation all plummeted. She shut her eyes for a moment. Just a moment. She reclined for a moment. Just a fleeting moment. Her legs, submerged in the water, felt quite alright. Her breathing slowed. Everything seemed fine, simply fine.

Sonny's eyes snapped open. Night had fallen. How long had she been unconscious? Or was it sleep?

8

Her leg, now numb, trailed behind as she attempted to inch toward the Prospector. Rolling over, she resumed her slow crawl. In the darkness, she reached the canoe. Her hand floundered inside for a snack bar but found nothing. In the uncertainty of the night, Sonny groped for the red dry-bag. "A strap!" She tugged it toward her, patting the sides until her fingers stumbled upon her secret stash. Tearing into the plastic wrapper, she crammed half the bar into her mouth. The rich, gooey chocolate, sweet and decadent, melted under the warmth of her tongue. The satisfying sensation of her molars grinding down the larger chunks was a delight she hadn't experienced in a while. That last bit of sustenance could carry her through the moment. The sensation of satiety tricked her mind into believing she had more reserves than she actually did.

She recalled an episode of RadioLab she and Mitch had once tuned into. It was about ultra-runners who deceived their bodies with a few drops of sugar water to endure the long nights. It was all a matter of the mind leading and the body following. That was an enjoyable long weekend with Mitch. Before the sadness, late nights, quarrels, and complications set in.

As she savored the final traces of chocolate sliding down her throat, she considered the second half of the protein bar. She ought to save it for the morning, ration her meals. But hadn't she earned this? If there was ever a moment in her life when she deserved a treat, it was now. A little nibble, a long lick of the outside—how she wanted to cheat. Logic intervened. There might be a more desperate moment between now and then when this meager sustenance would be vital. And so, she rewrapped the remaining half in its plastic shield. She tucked it into her pocket where the useless satellite beacon should have found a home but was now only dead weight.

Had the sun recently set? How long till morning? She reached into the red dry-bag again and pulled out her phone. She switched it on, watching the boot-up graphics. No bars. No signal. The clock read a quarter past nine. She had been out for a good six hours, lying half on the trail, half in the river. The next question was whether to relieve herself in the dry suit or attempt to remove it in time.

There was no modesty. Who would she be modest around? In one of the articles she read, it said she was more likely to meet a moose than a human on the river. The chainsaw man may have exceeded those chances.

She tugged at the hook and loop fastener to access the XX heavy-duty zipper. Billy had waxed the zipper for her in the store. It should move with ease. The dry suit was now loose. Billy's advice had proven invaluable. She'd been comfortable throughout the trip thanks to all this gear.

With her trusty paddle in her good hand, Sonny steadied herself. Her fingers traced the gunwale of the canoe until she found herself upright. Rising on her uninjured foot, she tested her weight. A good sign—not broken.

She fished out the little red flashlight from her pocket, the one with the magnetic end and hat clip. Sonny pulled the hat string tight. It had been dangling around her neck since she lost her ball cap at launch. She put it on, mindful of the makeshift bandage. The flashlight's clip slid onto the brim of the hat, providing a guiding light in the night that freed her hands. Now she could see where she was going.

The pressure began to mount. With careful deliberation, she moved toward the nearest tree sizable enough to bear her weight. The forest teemed with such trees. She faced away from the tree, letting her dry suit and hiking pants fall to the ground, followed by her underwear. Closing her eyes and taking a deep breath, Sonny leaned backward in a trust fall against the tree. The angle was steeper than anticipated and awkward. She adjusted her footing until it felt right. The ensuing release was the most satisfying sensation she could recall. The only sound was that of liquid hitting the ground, clear of her dry suit.

The relief, the sugar from the protein bar, and the accomplishment of those first steps filled her with renewed determination. "I can do this. I will make it," she assured herself. Reality intruded soon enough. The toilet paper was in the blue barrel. She was leaning against a tree without the strength, or the means, to stand back up. Any attempt might further injure her ankle. She couldn't risk dropping the paddle. She couldn't bend down to retrieve her pants or dry suit without it. Yet the flashlight still worked. She could see all the other trees she hadn't chosen. They stood silent and indifferent in the darkness. Looking down, she noticed the base of the tree sloped. Everything had run down, pooling at the bottom where the dry suit, pants, and panties rested. Gravity always wins. "Get back up," she murmured to the spirits of the woods. It was her mantra for her daughters, and a reminder for herself.

Positioning the edge of her paddle at the base of the tree, she pushed forward as if to take a powerful stroke, leaning ahead. The combined effort managed to lift her off the tree. As her instinct to stand upright took over, the pain returned. The splint held fast, aiding her to her feet. Bending at the knee, she stooped. Extracting her emergency knife, she cut the waistband of her $39 panties. She flung the sodden cotton into the wilderness. With her pants pulled up, she was going commando. Pulling the dry suit back on, her arms slid into the sleeves. Warmth crept back into her body. Paddle in hand, Sonny made her way back to the Prospector 14.

This was the reality she had signed up for. She was aware of the risks, the harrowing tales, yet she had thought this was a good idea. This was her fight now, alone in the wilderness. "I can do this, right?"

9

Billy had given it to her straight. Dragging the canoe was a big no-no. Yes, there were some good types of scratches on the hull that would testify to the adventure she would endure. Those were trophies of accomplishment. Rocks and branches in the water could do that. But there were also some nasty marks that could weaken the hull, rip the gel coat right off the thing. Those were the marks of the idiot—the idiot who dragged their canoe over land instead of taking the time to portage it; hoist it up on their shoulders like a real outdoors person. That was the right way. Billy had high expectations for Sonny, but now she was looking like a first-rate idiot.

All that mattered was the blue barrel. Sonny refused to get distracted by time or the darkness. She held the paddle in her good hand like a prized possession, while her bad hand clutched the bow deck handle. Lifting with her legs, she propelled the Prospector forward, one step at a time. The sound of friction on the dirt and pine needles filled the air, interrupted only by the occasional rough crunch of roots or the thud of the canoe dropping. She kept moving forward.

Sonny resisted the urge to look at her phone or check her watch. Time had no meaning in this universe. Only the blue barrel mattered. Her head turns and steps revealed a world that existed only in 50-yard slices, illuminated by the 1500 lumen light on her head. The reflective eyes of creatures watched her from the darkness, surprised by this crazy woman trying to prove herself. She imagined their thoughts before they galloped or crawled away. She entertained the idea of capturing a few of them, lashing them together, and training them to carry her forward. Such thoughts were distractions from the pain.

Many of these mammals were thirsty, longing for cool water from the river. But strange Sonny scared them off, and so she continued on alone, focused on reaching the blue barrel.

The world began to expand, unfolding between the dawning light and the enclosing darkness. Sonny's flashlight seemed less significant. The river resurged into her perception, its roar and murmurs trickling over the rocks. The water's motion was dominant, surging along its meandering course with tremendous force. Sonny had passed the halfway point where she had fallen, unnoticed. The smooth pine and earth path, the rough terrain with jutting branches where her canoe scraped and pushed forward, consumed her attention and focus. She hadn't imagined completing the journey in one go. But there it was.

"Where's the barrel?" she questioned the spirits, as though they would even bother to answer. The canoe now returned to the Two-Hearted, she surveyed the surroundings with her light to find evidence of a bear. The blue barrel had disappeared in the countless hours. *No point in calling for it like a lost pet*, she thought. Her phone had no signal; not even a tracker would do any good. She hobbled into the dark, ten yards from the trail, pursuing what she believed to be tracks.

The trail began with the bag holding the rope and pulleys. A few yards away, her tent and poles rested, followed by the hammock, stove, and medical kit. With the flashlight now in hand, she scanned the woods, but nothing else came into view. A few more steps, another scan at the edges of the light, nothing else.

She could feel her energy wane. Her enthusiasm was on a quick decline without finding more food. "Take only memories, leave only footprints," she muttered. Sonny bent down to pick up the litter the thief left behind. She traced her steps back, collecting each item, until she reached the rope and pulleys. From there, she gazed at the first light of morning reflecting on the water. Beyond it, in the distance, she imagined Lake Superior's pink and blue skies. Gulls and terns danced against the ceaseless winds.

She went first for the painkillers in the medical kit, the ones prescribed to Mitch in his final days. The ones that the pharmacist had reminded her not to flush or discard down the sink or toilet. The ones she had tossed in the kit "just in case." She swallowed two with water. After a while, she realized the pain persisted, but she didn't care. She didn't give a damn about her leg or wrist, the things she needed to do to survive, or how many days had passed. She recalled the half snack bar in her pocket as she fumbled with the zipper, then fumbled to unwrap it. It remained intact, warmed by the heat of her body during the night's journey. As she sat on a log, gazing across the river's expanse, she pondered when would be the ideal moment to consume it. Famished, was it enough to warrant devouring it? Or should she save it for later? As the drug-induced apathy continued to grow, gravity seized hold of the snack bar, causing it to plummet to the earth, mingling with the soil and pine. She looked down to where it fell. A lithe brown chipmunk bolted toward her. It snatched the remnants and dashed off five feet before turning to face her. The plucky creature nibbled away at the bar's edges for a spell. She couldn't catch it even if she desired to, and she had no intention of doing anything but sit there. Sonny reminisced about the chocolate from the night before. She thought on the caramel's gooeyness and the nuttiness's crunch. Her mouth began to water, and spittle sprayed out as she cried out, "Hey, that's mine!" But it was too little, too late.

Her words reverberated to the world, sending the rodent scurrying into the dark woods.

The rough surface of the log proved to be far from hospitable. Exhausted, she yearned for slumber. So she gathered her belongings and stowed them inside the canoe. Instead of preparing for departure downstream, she fashioned a cozy sanctuary by arranging her possessions into a makeshift bed. She then nestled herself atop it and descended into sleep, asking, "Will I ever be the same as before?"

10

The world materialized before her, regaining its recognizable form. It appeared distant and hazy; was it "the dream?" Male voices murmured in the background, engaged in a conversation about fish. Sonny became aware of her surroundings. With effort, she pried open her crusty eyelids, revealing a timber beam ceiling. She found herself lying in a bed. Attempting to turn her head proved futile. Was she tied down? Captive?

"Looks like Snow White has finally awakened from her slumber," quipped the muffled voice of a man.

Leaning over her, a man's face came into view, peering down at her. "Hello, Ms. White. I'm Doc. That one's Bashful, and the other is Sleazy."

The other voice corrected, "Sneezy!"

"I... I can't turn my head to see them," Sonny managed to respond.

"We've immobilized your neck and bandaged your head. You had a substantial bump when we found you," explained the man.

"Where am I?" Sonny inquired, her voice filled with confusion.

"You are in the finest established hunting cabin in the Great Lakes. I am Pike, and the other voices you hear belong to Riker," the man replied.

"Hello, ma'am," Riker added.

"And the other one is Ranger," Pike continued.

A mumble escaped Ranger's mouth, resembling a greeting of sorts.

"What happened? How did I end up here?" Sonny asked, her curiosity piqued.

"We were about to ask you the same thing. How are you feeling?" Pike questioned, concern lacing his voice.

Pike placed a small flashlight in front of her, examining each of her eyes. "I must say, you have beautiful eyes to match that stunning hematoma," he remarked, before clicking off the light. "Riker, I'm going to remove the cervical collar."

"I concur, doc," Riker agreed.

Sonny breathed a sigh of relief. "Oh, thank God, a doctor," she uttered.

"Well, not technically a doctor, ma'am," he walked back the comment. "But the honorable members of the U.S.

Marine Corps ensured I received training for medical emergencies," Pike clarified.

A ripping sound resonated in the air as the hook and loop fasteners of the restraint were undone.

She felt Pike's weight shift as he settled on the edge of the bed beside her. "Just relax," he reassured her with a soothing and charming voice. "I'll check a few things while you lie there." His rough fingers touched her wrist, assessing her pulse. It had been quite some time since anyone had touched her.

"Please open your mouth."

Sonny complied.

"And close."

Another click, and the light returned, now focused on her injury instead of her eyes. "Nice stitching, Riker. Clean," Pike complimented as a beep signaled in the background. Within seconds, a series of beeps followed. He prompted her to open her mouth, allowing Pike to retrieve the thermometer. "Normal temp. Ms. White, your dwarfs are delighted to report that you're going to be fine," Pike informed her.

"Please, call me Sonny. Seems like I'm gonna run out of 'thank yous' with you three," she remarked.

"Sonny. Huh? I thought you'd smile more with a name like that."

"Yeah, most people make that mistake."

"Well, you're gonna be fine, Sonny," Pike reassured her. "You can sit up if you want, but take it slow and easy."

Assisting her, Pike helped Sonny sit up and swing her legs over the edge of the bed. She found herself in a rustic hunting shack. A single room adorned with postcards, photographs, advertisements, pin-up girls, Skoal tin lids, and calendars covering most of the timber. It seemed like the place was built and decorated starting in the 1920s. "You boys look a little too young for the likes of Betty Grable, don't you think?"

"Betty Grable. Nice gams," remarked Ranger.

"Betty Boop, what a dish," replied Pike.

Sonny's curiosity piqued as she tried to recall how she ended up here. "How did I get here? Last I remember, a chipmunk was making off with my granola bar."

"That must have been one helluva chipper to give you a goose egg like that," Ranger quipped.

"No." Sonny's brow furrowed at the odd thought. "The chipmunk didn't—"

"I was about to say, that sounds rather unlikely," Pike interjected.

"I've been traveling the Two-Hearted River these past few days. You know, taking in the scenery and whatnot. Then, out of the blue, I stumble and take a nasty tumble, twisting my ankle and bashing my noggin. And, well, I suppose you stumbled upon me in that sorry state," Sonny explained.

"We couldn't help but notice your crafty ankle adornment. I took the liberty of replacing it with a shiny aluminum version. Our astute comrade Riker stumbled upon a mysterious blue barrel bobbing its way downstream, filled to the brim with all sorts of goodies. With his years of skills and training, he tracked its origin upstream, and lo and behold, there you were, out, lost in dreamland," Pike stated.

"We used your canoe as a stretcher to carry you here," finally spoke Riker.

"Well, Riker and I carried you. Ranger here isn't ready to shoulder that burden. He's still a growing boy," Pike said, glancing at Ranger.

"Hey, is that a short joke?" Ranger responded, standing up from the card table.

"Whoa." Sonny realized that he hadn't been standing that whole time. When he did straighten up, he had to stoop to avoid hitting his head on the rafters. "You're quite tall."

"Straight and to the point. I appreciate that in a woman," Pike quipped. "Ranger stands at a towering six feet, seven inches, Sonny. He's part of the 'less than one percent' in the world."

"You don't give him one of those ironic nicknames like Tiny? Shorty?" Sonny inquired.

"Nah, nah, they called me that in the Army. I don't go for that shit," Ranger replied.

"Riker and I call him Ranger. He served in the Army, where the boys go to play war. Marines have to live it," Pike taunted like an older brother.

"Well, military humor," Sonny replied. "Thank you for carrying me here. And thank you for finding me."

"Riker, why don't you rustle up some grub?" Pike suggested. "Our guest must be starved from fighting off wild chipmunks. You stay put for a while," he instructed Sonny. "Take it easy, okay?" Pike rose and made his way to the other end of the cabin, 15 feet away, near the door where a 1950s-era refrigerator and gas stove stood.

"I'm fine, I assure you," Sonny responded.

"Indulge me, please. When was the last time someone served you a meal in bed?" Pike implored with a playful smile.

Ranger, leisurely leaning against the crossbeam of the rafters like a child in a jungle gym, watched her and asked, "Sonny, what's a nice lady like you doing solo on the Two-Hearted? Couldn't wait for the summer tour?"

"It's quite obvious, she wanted to avoid those blood-sucking mosquitoes," Pike interjected.

"I despise mosquitoes. That's one thing we share," Ranger replied. "You wanna talk about bug bites, try Fort Jackson in June. Bug bites and sunburn. Whoa-boy. I tell ya."

"Right here, in the spring, we have mosquitoes and black flies the size of bats. Nothing worse. That's why we're here in May," Pike explained.

"That's the reason?" Ranger queried.

"That, and the fish," Pike added.

"Yeah, yeah, fish," Ranger responded.

"Did you boys manage to catch anything?" Sonny inquired.

"Riker landed five steelhead and three brook trout," Pike said, handing Sonny a cup of water and taking a seat on the lower bunk across from her. "Ranger got ten steelhead, and I hooked seven trout."

"Is that considered good?" Sonny asked.

Pike shrugged nonchalantly. "Depends. I was using a Hare's Ear, while Ranger had the Elk Hair. What were you casting, Riker?"

"They call it a Grannom," Riker replied.

"You threw your Grandma?" Pike quipped.

"Grannom, not Grandma," Riker clarified.

"Now, let me tell you something about Riker. That old soul is quite the expert when it comes to tossing grandmas." Pike spoke low, a knowing smile on his face, aware that Riker would catch his words. With a charismatic grin directed at Sonny, he posed a pointed question, "So, Sonny, are you truly interested in delving into the intricacies of fishing? Or, perchance, are you attempting to sidestep Ranger's inquiry?" Pike's expression carried a mischievous charm.

"What was the question?" Sonny feigned innocence.

Pike, undeterred, revealed the lingering inquiry with a playful tone, "Ah, the burning question on all our minds is, 'What's a nice girl like you doing in a place like this?'"

As if on cue, Ranger slid over to join Pike on the lower bunk, contorting to fit, offering a bottle of water to Sonny. "Bottle of water?" he suggested, his presence adding to the camaraderie of the moment.

"She's already got one water," Pike interjected, but Ranger persisted, insisting, "You can never have too much water."

Grateful for the gesture, Sonny responded, "Thank you" with a smile, as she cracked open the bottle and indulged in a long, refreshing sip. "I suppose I was more parched than I realized."

Pike's grin widened, displaying his gleaming set of teeth, as he responded with a touch of wit, "In the Marines, we have a technical term for that. It's called dehydration." His words carried a suave and charming tone, devoid of any sarcasm that might have been impolite coming from someone else.

However, the conversation took a heartfelt turn as Sonny opened up, sharing her personal truth. "I am a recent widow," she revealed, her voice carrying a delicate blend of vulnerability and resilience. "For the past two years, I stood faithfully by my husband's side, observing the gradual decline of his health, feeling utterly powerless. We shared countless conversations, always nurturing a glimmer of hope that we would embark on new adventures together, fulfilling the retirement dreams we never had the opportunity to pursue. Mitch, my late husband, possessed a deep admiration for Ernest Hemingway. We actually met at a book club where we bonded over our shared love for literature. He was particularly into Hemingway's works. Mitch would often revisit Hemingway's writings. Over the years, we saved and meticulously planned our journey to retrace the author's footsteps on a safari, envisioning a rainy springtime in Paris, and even daring to run with the bulls in Pamplona, Spain."

Pondering the question posed by Ranger, Sonny paused for a moment before responding, "You see, I came to the secluded woods of Michigan for my own Hemingway-inspired adventure. In 1925, Hemingway published a collection of short stories titled 'In Our Time.' One of the stories, 'Big Two-Hearted River,' portrays his character traveling to Seney, Michigan to fish after the war."

Ranger interjected, "But we're nowhere near Seney."

Sonny nodded. "You're right. The story actually takes place on the Fox River, where Hemingway's character fishes for trout. I read in an article from the time that the good people of Newberry wanted to write Hemingway a letter clearly explaining. But Two-Hearted sounds better; it's poetry, has meaning. The entire area around Seney was ravaged by fire in the 1890s. It reminded Hemingway of Italy, bombed out. In the first part of the story, he alludes to the war, discussing it indirectly. And in the second part, he engages in grasshopper hunting as a means to fish, again addressing the war indirectly."

"The theory of omission," Riker chimed in.

Sonny smiled, acknowledging his input. "Exactly. Hemingway masterfully describes themes of home, friendship, and family, as well as the profound impact of war, all without explicitly stating, 'Hey, I'm dealing with the aftermath of war,' all before it was even referred to as PTSD."

Ranger, captivated by the conversation, exclaimed, "Whoa, I definitely need to read this story. Which war was this? Vietnam?"

"The Great War, World War I."

"War is never great," Riker said just loud enough to be heard. "Do you have any allergies? I probably should have asked that ten minutes ago."

Sonny replied, "No, no allergies."

Pike chimed in, his tone half-joking, "Was hitting your head and twisting your ankle in the middle of nowhere on your to-do list? Or perhaps only canoeing down a frigid river with rapids in the spring? Both sound pretty darn dangerous to me."

Sonny responded, her voice filled with a mix of nostalgia and resignation, "It was all talk, just talk. Then, after my husband's passing... well..."

Pike suggested, "Most people would consider taking a cruise."

"Ha," Sonny explained. "Well, I bought a canoe and a paddle and drove eight hours north. That's how I ended up here."

Ranger remarked, "That's a bitchin' canoe you've got. Salesman must have made his nut on that one."

Pike interjected with a reprimand, "Dude! Using 'nut' in front of a lady? Haven't they taught you anything in the Army?" He then turned to Sonny, offering an apology, "Please accept my apologies, Sonny. He was raised by skink lizards."

Sonny smiled appreciatively. "It's been a faithful canoe, more like a companion, really. Its name is Prospector 14, and we've been through a lot this week."

Pike added with a hint of pride, "Sally—my rifle—and I share that kind of relationship."

Riker agreed, "Same here. Mine is called Daphne Blake."

Pike explained, "He has a thing for redheads."

Sonny, slightly taken aback, said, "Right..." unsure of how to respond to the banter. "That salesman, Billy, knew his stuff when it came to the equipment."

The clattering sound of a spoon hitting a plate emerged from the kitchen, and Riker announced, "Okay," as he walked over with a plate and handed it to Sonny. He then squeezed onto the lower bunk beside Ranger, pushing him into Pike. From his shirt pocket, Riker produced a fork and knife wrapped in a napkin, then handed them to Sonny.

"Thank you," Sonny expressed her gratitude. Glancing at the three boys piled on top of each other in the lower bunk a foot away, she realized they were watching her intently as she was about to eat. "Eggs?" she inquired.

"Yeah, I figured, easy, fast, protein, mix in some vegetables. Those mushrooms, hand-picked and fresh. Did you know that the world's largest mushroom is right here in Michigan?" Riker shared.

"I think I've heard something about that," Sonny responded with a smile, enjoying the first bite of her meal. Holding back from shoveling the food in her mouth from the feeling of being famished, she sounded her satisfaction, "Mmm, it's delicious." Curiosity sparked within her, leading her to inquire, "Are you boys married? Do you leave any hunting widows behind each season?"

The three exchanged glances before Pike answered, "Not married. Ranger went on a date last year."

Ranger, with a touch of vulnerability in his voice, explained, "Ya know how things are. You get together, desperate to find if they meet, like, eighty percent of what you're looking for, and ya always feel like you're never quite good enough. She's got standards, see. And they end up finding someone else. Women today have high standards. No offense, ma'am."

Sonny responded with understanding, "None taken. Men don't have it easy. I've watched my daughters go through a string of boys. Each one supposedly better than the last, but never quite measuring up to some unrealistic expectation. Until one day, they found the 'right guy.' It took a long time. I used to say, 'He's a nice boy, treats you right, seems like a keeper.' But they would say, 'Mom, I'm not settling for just anyone. Did you settle for Dad?' Mitch told them, 'I was lucky to get your mom.' And I said, 'I was lucky to find your dad.' I can still vividly recall that conversation, sitting around the dining room table. The girls had graduated from university, very popular and sought after. But Sundays were reserved for family, and they always made sure to show up so I could feed them. They waited, both of them, for a long time. Boy after boy until my sons-in-law showed up at the table one Sunday. To be honest, my sons-in-law are both not the greatest. They may have impressive jobs, good backgrounds, and a certain social status, but they don't treat my daughters, well, right. As a parent, I can't help but wonder where I went wrong. But then I remember, it's their life," Sonny reflected, her voice carrying a mix of parental concern and acceptance.

Riker interjected, "You gave them the training and tools, but ultimately, it's up to them to carry out the mission."

"Yes, yes, exactly," Sonny agreed. "Are you from the area? I read an article where some downstate 'trolls' came to the Two-Hearted to fish and got into trouble. They were supposed to have known what to do, but when some local boys from Newberry found them, they were desperate. Nearly clinging to the Newberry boys, the locals had to give up their fishing trip, insisting they get them out of the woods and back to civilization."

"I'm from Berkley," Pike started. "These two are from Royal Oak."

Riker asked, "What other aid or comfort can we provide?"

"Too far, too far. Sounds like a porno," Ranger chided.

11

Riker carefully added two more quarters of split log to the sturdy cast iron stove. Sonny, ensconced within the cozy confines of the room, drew a deep breath, relishing the warmth and dryness in the air. It was a rare moment of comfort for her, reminiscent of the days spent in that Newberry hotel room. Her attention drifted to Pike and Ranger, engaged in a spirited game of cards, their playful banter echoing the camaraderie of mischievous boys. They jested and challenged each other, staking their claims of dominance in the pack.

"In this vast expanse of nature, Sonny, what drove you here?" Riker inquired, his voice carrying a thoughtful timbre.

"Some *Eat, Pray, Love* shit?" Ranger interjected.

"Language," Pike gently admonished.

"What?" Ranger retorted.

"The title is nefarious," Pike said.

"I wasn't particularly fond of the book, so no, no *Eat, Pray, Love* shit," Sonny replied. "In Gilbert's book, she abandons her partner for a younger man. The story promises self-reflection and rising above her circumstances, but ultimately, she finds herself entangled with another man."

Ranger's eyes widened at Sonny's words. "So, not a fan of men?"

"On the contrary, I have great affection for men," Sonny clarified, her voice carrying the weight of experience. "I've been fortunate to have many exceptional men in my life. But Gilbert's story speaks to the human condition. She traverses the lives of these men—committed, casual, and everything in between—only to end up in the same place. What troubles me is that she overlooks two crucial aspects. First, the man she left behind was superior in many ways to the one she ends up with."

"Stand by your man," Pike said.

"Tammy Wynette, 1968," Riker replied.

Sonny continued, "And second, she brushes aside the fact that real people cannot simply abandon everything and embark on a worldwide search for 'the answer.' Gilbert indulges in extensive introspection about the world's impoverished yet content inhabitants, all while failing to acknowledge the privilege of evading the burdens of everyday life."

"Kind of like buying an expensive canoe?" Pike interjected, a touch of dry wit in his voice.

"Valid point," Sonny conceded. "Not everyone can afford to splurge five thousand dollars on a boat."

"Five grand? Fuck me!" Ranger exclaimed, his eyes widening in disbelief. "Don't let me touch that thing, I'd break it."

"I have no plans for an *Eat, Pray, Love* escapade. No Oprah endorsements in the works," Sonny affirmed, her conviction ringing clear. "I'm just trying to get away from things—something."

Riker settled into a plush armchair near the stove, eyeing the metal wood bin. In a swift motion, he lifted the entire bin effortlessly and opened the stove door. With a flick of his wrist, he revealed a glimmering blade. Riker exuded an air of quiet competence—a man who could tackle any situation. With a discerning eye, he selected a split piece of wood and began to whittle it with graceful strokes, sending slivers and chips cascading onto the stove's door.

"That book somehow foreshadowed a disconcerting aspect of our culture," Sonny ventured, her voice filled with contemplation. "When I was young, Sundays meant attending church. I don't know if that was your experience as well, but it was mine. And to this day, that spiritual connection remains important to me. Yet I've noticed that the pews grow emptier, and the path to the choicest seats becomes easier."

"Times change, Sonny. It's the way of the world," Pike offered, his voice tinged with acceptance, laying down a card.

"Maybe. I see people still yearning for that connection, but instead of finding solace in churches, they seek tribes in spin classes, workplaces, gaming communities, or various social groups. It seems to me that while a gym trainer may excel at cardio, they may not possess the aptitude to offer spiritual guidance for grief counseling or infidelity."

"You've sought solace in group therapy?" Pike asked.

"A circle of folding chairs in a chilly basement, baring my soul to strangers—I've lived through that cliché of support groups recently," Sonny replied, her tone tinged with a mixture of weariness and resilience.

There was a moment of understanding and shared experience between them, as the weight of vulnerability hung in the air. The trials and tribulations of seeking healing and connection echoed true.

"How did we get on this topic?" Ranger asked.

"*Eat, Pray, Love.* Let her speak," Riker interjected, his tone encouraging.

"There's an abundance of groups one can join, tribes to be a part of, packs to run with," Sonny continued.

"God. Family. Country. Corps!" Pike barked.

"OO-RAH. Semper Fidelis," Riker responded instinctively.

"Yes, those crucial circles. God, family first, with a select few worthy friends. It's an exclusive circle. And the North Star of it all isn't found at work or in an adventure-seeking expedition club. Nowadays, people seem drawn to the allure of through-hiking—the Pacific Crest Trail or the Appalachian Trail. They traverse thousands of miles, yearning for extraordinary experiences and hoping to find a connection. This kind of spiritual quest used to find its home in churches, temples, or devasthanas..."

"Fifty-cent word, Sonny," Pike playfully commented.

"It means a Hindu place of worship," Sonny clarified.

"Roger that."

"But now, that community support is scattered. Even the coffee shop down the street seems to serve as a quasi-sanctuary for a group of regulars, treating it as a sacred space for grounded beans."

"A good cup of coffee is hard to come by," Pike added with a chuckle.

"It's the circle, and we should count ourselves blessed to have it. Because when it's gone, well, it's gone," Sonny concluded, her voice laced with a sense of finality.

Pike, Riker, and Ranger grasped the essence of Sonny's words—loss and the arduous journey of recovery.

Breaking the silence, Riker posed a question. "Have you ever heard of the Camino de Santiago?"

The three companions shook their heads in unison.

"It's an ancient trail," Riker began, his voice carrying a hint of wonder. "It starts in France, winds its way through Spain, and culminates at the majestic Atlantic Ocean. The Romans used to follow the path of the Milky Way, considering it a route to the world's end. What started as a mere trade route eventually became intertwined with the legend of Saint James and his sacred pilgrimage to Santiago de Compostela—a stunning church near the ocean." Riker paused in his whittling, lifting his gaze to the heavens as if seeking inspiration. "In Hebrews 11:13, there's a passage that says, 'These all died in faith, not having received the promises, but having seen them afar off, and were persuaded of them, and embraced them, and confessed that they were strangers and pilgrims on the Earth.'" Riker returned his focus to the wood in his hands, carving away with careful precision. "Those who embarked on this journey were known as pilgrims—sinners in search of penance. Today, nearly half a million people walk this path they call The Way. Each one carries a unique purpose, a different reason that compels them to tread its hallowed ground. They seek answers, hoping to find them along The Way or at its end."

"Do they find what they're looking for?" Sonny inquired, her voice filled with hope.

"Few find it on The Way itself," Riker replied, his words carrying a note of melancholy.

"Oh," Sonny responded, a hint of disappointment tinging her tone.

"Instead, they discover it upon returning home or attempting to reintegrate into their ordinary lives. I've met some pilgrims. Their eyes hold a distant gaze, forever scanning the horizon, longing to be back on that trail. The journey changes them, down to their very core, transforming every cell of their being along The Way. No matter how hard they try, the only way to truly return is to walk the path once more. They strive to live honorable lives, to become better versions of themselves, but it's only on the trail, during their quest, that they experience a sense of completeness. There's no grand revelation at the trail's end or a magical transformation brought about by their deeds. It's the journey itself that holds the key."

"Have you walked The Way?" Sonny asked, curiosity dancing in her voice.

"Not yet. Perhaps one day," Pike responded, his words tinged with wistful longing.

"It sounds utterly fascinating," Sonny remarked, her voice filled with awe.

"'The sharp edge of a razor is difficult to pass over; thus the wise say the path to Salvation is hard,'" Riker quoted, his voice resonating with wisdom.

"Where is that from?" Pike inquired.

"It's a passage from the Upanishads, an ancient religious text. The conundrum you're describing, Sonny, is not a new one. It's the query that haunts any awakened soul." Riker lifted the carving to reveal two links of chain perfectly crafted from the split log. "Sonny, do you recall the word 'timshel' from *East of Eden*? 'Thou mayest.' Everything is your choice."

12

She woke last, stepped out first. They were readying for her return to the Two-Hearted. Riker cleaned the stove of its remnants of breakfast. Ranger packed, methodical and silent. Pike swept, a futile stand against the encroaching mice in the old camp.

At the break of dawn, each bead of dew clung precariously to the emerald pine needles, trembling under the kiss of the rising sun. Each droplet, a tiny prism, reflected the morning light, setting the forest ablaze in a cascade of crystalline brilliance. The woodland expanse shimmered in an ethereal ballet of dancing diamonds, receding into the velvety distance where the eye dared not tread.

A chilly zephyr whispered through the expanse of pine, carrying with it the promise of a new day. Every exhalation painted the frost-kissed air with the gossamer ghost of breath, a fleeting testament to life amidst the sacred silence. It was a spectacle of beauty so profound it snatched the breath from Sonny's lungs, an orchestra of light and shadow conducted by the whims of the sun.

This wonderland exacted a toll, paid not in coin but in the currency of the road less traveled: each scrap, scrape, and scar a voucher of the journey. Yet, as she let the words, "It's worth it" slip from her lips, they hung in the air for a brief moment before dissolving into the ether, a whispered testament to the beauty they bore witness to. A grand tapestry, woven from the threads of dawn's light and nature's quiet resilience, beckoned to the heart, inviting it to fall in love with the raw, unspoken poetry of the moment.

Pike's voice filled the air with a touch of reverence. "This sanctuary, nestled in the heart of North America's most fertile hunting and fishing grounds, was built by the hands of my grandfather and his brothers back in 1911. They carved out this piece of paradise, a refuge against the world's harsh realities."

His eyes took on a faraway look. "After returning from the trenches of Europe in 1918, the elder brothers would navigate a Duesenberg through the forest's maze. The younger ones, they came back from the Second World War in the late '40s, steering a Ford Mercury Woody through this very wilderness. Their spirits are etched into the woodwork, their stories whispered by the wind through the trees."

A warm smile spread across Pike's face. "I continue to

tend to this place, keeping it alive, preserving the legacy. And the dream—well, the dream is to share this slice of heaven with my own kids one day. To have them understand the rich mosaic of their history, the resilience and dreams of their forefathers, and their deep, unbroken connection with this magical place. That's the ultimate dream, isn't it?"

"That's a nice dream," Sonny replied.

The sharp slam of the screen door jolted the quiet morning as Ranger swaggered out onto the front porch. His weight elicited a chorus of groans from the wooden boards beneath him. Unleashing a hearty belch, he grinned. "What? It's a compliment in some cultures."

Pike retorted dryly, "Maybe, but not in ours."

As the last vestiges of Riker's bustle in the kitchen echoed into silence, he emerged to join them outside.

"Are you sure about this, Sonny?" Pike asked, his voice laced with concern.

"I have to finish. I need to make it to the end. I can handle it," Sonny responded, her eyes blazing with determination.

Riker flashed her an encouraging grin. "I have no doubt you can, Sonny."

Meanwhile, Ranger strode over to the plastic tarp and whipped it off with a swift yank, scattering morning dew droplets in a shimmering spray. The droplets sprinkled down on the rest of the group, shimmering like stardust in the early morning light.

With a soft punch to Ranger's shoulder, Riker grinned. "You know, slower can sometimes be faster."

"It's just water," Ranger shrugged.

"It is just water," Riker conceded.

The sight of Riker next to Ranger brought the enormity of their task into sharp relief. Riker, at a meager five-foot-six, was dwarfed by Ranger's towering frame. With a gentle pat of Ranger's shoulder, Riker directed, "We've got this one. Why don't you take the rear and keep an eye out for bears?"

Sonny checked the blue barrel, snapping the lid shut. It contained only a quarter of what she'd started with. She hoisted it over her first shoulder, then wiggled it onto the second. Meanwhile, Ranger effortlessly hoisted the red dry-bag, making it seem as light as a balloon.

Pike and Riker fell into synchronization, carefully lifting and turning the green vessel overhead. Sonny followed behind, stepping gingerly on her tender foot. Ranger brought up the rear, rifle slung over one shoulder, red bag dangling from his hand.

The trail was a mix of dark gray sand and black dirt, a historical reminder, as Pike explained, of the forest fire in 1871, the same year as the Great Chicago Fire. Trees from this region were harvested to rebuild the city that burned. These tall trees, only one hundred and fifty years old, were mere children in the grand timescale of nature. "Any fan of Tolkien would know the importance of trees," he remarked.

Sonny noticed the lack of tree roots on this path

compared to the one that had tripped her. Pike shared his thoughts, "I bet that's because this path was made and walked frequently as the forest grew alongside it. The river trail is a lot wilder, with fewer people until recent years."

The realization that she had never been more than half a mile from people this entire trip was comforting. The wilderness was dotted with good people, like Pike, Riker, and Ranger, who shared a deep connection with the forest and its rich history.

Upon reaching the river, Pike handed Sonny a piece of paper. "These are our email addresses and phone numbers. Don't hesitate to use them if you need anything," he said.

Touched by their generosity, Sonny hugged each of them in turn. Every "Thank you" was echoed by their "Yes ma'am." Recognizing the pattern, she teased, "Well, I better stop this infinite loop, or we'll be here all day."

Sonny slipped into the fresh dry suit. It took a little longer than the first day, but she got there. With a final tug at her vest straps, she stepped cautiously back into the canoe, balanced herself with her paddle, and sat down. She strained with the paddle, and with a mighty push from Ranger behind her, the canoe sprang into the cold river, swiftly carried downstream toward Lake Superior.

UNDER THE GENTLE propulsion of her practiced strokes, the Prospector surrendered to the playful whims of the current, making her journey downstream an unhurried waltz with nature. The familiar, soothing cadence of cool water lapping against her vessel felt like a serenade from an old friend, its lyrics an ode to solitude and tranquility.

Without warning, a swift shadow sliced through the air above her, momentarily veiling the glow of the morning sun. Barely a stone's throw ahead, a spectacle unfolded that made time lose all meaning. An American Bald Eagle, a creature steeped in majestic elegance and raw power, dramatically unfurled its broad wings, breaking its speed with an air of graceful defiance. It hung suspended for an eternal second before descending like an avenging angel.

Its sharp, gleaming yellow talons, like the fingers of a seasoned pianist striking a decisive chord, extended and decisively latched onto its unsuspecting prey. A robust steelhead, a magnificent specimen that easily weighed twenty pounds, if not more, was the chosen breakfast. The eagle's talons pressed into the distinctive pink stripe running along the steelhead's length, between the green-speckled belly and scaled, finned top, as if imprinting its claim for the world to see.

The bald eagle's great wings, patterned in hues of brown, beat the still morning air, a symphony of strength, dominance. Each flap, each wave, lifted it and its heavy bounty higher into the sky's limitless canvas.

The spectacle was so close that Sonny felt herself synchronized with the rhythm of each powerful flap, each beat a palpable force that echoed in her heart. She thought about Ranger, with his rugged strength, effortlessly wrestling such a fish from the river, while the others might falter. The sheer idea of wrestling such a gargantuan catch from the icy river depths seemed like a Herculean task. Yet, the eagle, in its primal elegance, made the feat look as simple as drawing breath. It ascended steadily, gaining momentum until it was a mere speck above the tree line, then disappeared from view.

A wave of wistfulness washed over Sonny. This ethereal moment... she yearned to share it with her best friend, Mitch. Her mind wandered to her phone; a quick snapshot would have immortalized the moment. Was it stowed away in the red dry-bag or the blue barrel? But the thought came and passed too late. She mused about capturing the serene river or the emerald tree line, then narrating the thrilling eagle encounter. There was no shortage of fish tales in the world, but this encounter, this story... would others believe her story?

Mitch would have if he were here. Mitch.

The icy tendrils of fear crept upon Sonny, as swift and merciless as the eagle's dive. A sudden apprehension seized her—a dread that she might never have another soul to share her stories with. The stark prospect of a life shrouded in loneliness, of an existence devoid of shared laughter and silent companionship, terrified her more than she could express. It echoed the empty weeks since Mitch had passed, his absence a void she was yet to fathom.

When Mitch had been ambushed by the first stroke, he was left a shadow of his once active self, confined to a walker. The second, more vicious stroke ravaged his ability to communicate, consigning him to the unforgiving confines of a hospital bed in their back living room. Sonny watched, helpless and tormented, as the man she loved disintegrated day by day, slipping away from her like grains of sand through clenched fingers. Each sunrise brought with it a heartbreaking subtraction, each sunset a painful reminder of the man she was losing. It was like witnessing a slow-burning fire consuming her most cherished possession, bit by agonizing bit, until nothing but ashes remained.

At times, the enormity of their suffering made her wish for a merciful end. This guilt-laden thought haunted her, lacing her prayers with desperation. Yet, the spark in Mitch's eyes on the better days, the familiar touch, the whispered endearments all kept her tethered to the hope that the man she loved was still there, buried beneath the layers of his affliction. Oh, he made her feel so good. And there were moments of confusion when he would ask to be taken to his truck. He needed to get to the truck. Only now did she realize that in his truck, sitting under the passenger seat, was the path to freedom taken by Hemingway.

This was the fear. The stark loneliness that yawned

before her, an unending chasm devoid of the love and companionship she had spent a lifetime cultivating. The family she had built with Mitch was a reflection of what once was, now their daughters enveloped in their own lives and loves. The past 24 hours spent in the warm company of three men had been a welcome distraction from her solitary existence. The fear whispered again, insidious and daunting, questioning her ability to find love and companionship again, warning of the potential pitfall of settling for less than what she deserved.

The fear of loneliness was intertwined with the dread of compromising, of settling for a life that was bereft of the joy and love she had known. Of sharing her existence with someone who was merely tolerable, or worse, cruel. The fear of being stuck, of being trapped in a loveless situation like so many women she had heard of, was as palpable as the fear of loneliness.

The house she had once shared with Mitch was now a spectral mansion, every corner echoing with his laughter, every room haunted by his memory. The fear of stepping into the garage to discover an emotional hand grenade, triggering a fresh explosion of loss and longing—this was fear. Fear of facing another day, of confronting her own human frailty.

As Sonny drifted down the Two-Hearted, the sight of an eagle's nest, nestled in the sturdy embrace of a treetop, brought her a moment's peace. Her male eagle brought the hefty steelhead to the nest, and Sonny watched as the female eagle fed, assuring herself of the eggs nestled within. It represented continuity, the unbroken cycle of life and love. It was a future. It was their future, a testament to survival and hope.

"Mitch," she called out to the spirit world. "I don't know if you can hear me, but I need to get over this fear. Can you send help?"

13

As Sonny navigated the major tributary, the low, ominous rumble of truck tires on the loose rock was an auditory cue to her precise location. She was nearest to the Coast Guard Line Road, just at the river bend where rental outfitters often dropped families for a long day of paddling in summer. Her study of the area maps reassured her that no more portages were in store. "Long and easy" was what the canoe livery promised.

The river had become familiar, a dance partner whose moves she had finally learned. Its turns, the way the sun pestered her eyes, the moments of respite when the river bent another way—she had grown attuned to its rhythm. The morning light, with its fiery persistence, ceased to bother her by eleven each day, when the brim of her hat, perfectly angled, shielded her from its searing rays. She would sometimes catch herself straining her ears for the distant crash of waves, for the faintest echo of Gichigami, the Ojibwe name for the great expanse of Lake Superior that contained ten percent of the world's fresh water.

The change was abrupt, like crossing an invisible barrier. The river's surroundings shifted dramatically from the shadowy deep woods and rugged banks to a barren landscape reminiscent of lunar plains, marked by steep dunes and sparse vegetation.

The Duck Lake Fire of 2012 had descended upon the Upper Peninsula of Michigan with a ravaging fury reminiscent of the fiery emblem of devastation in Hemingway's prose. In his story "Big Two-Hearted River," his description of the devastation of war he witnessed in Europe was similar to the devastation to the area of Seney, along the Fox River. Nature, in its elemental form, had wrought destruction on a scale that dwarfed all life in its path, casting an eerie gloom that blanketed the landscape, transforming it into a nightmarish tableau of ashes and charred relics of what once was a vibrant ecosystem.

The verdant canvas of the Peninsula, once teeming with life, was replaced by an expanse of blackened tree skeletons that punctured the ash-gray sky. The scent of singed foliage and the mournful silence hung heavy in the air, the birds that once animated the forest with their calls were silenced, and the once frolicking animals were absent. The water of the Two-Hearted, which had always mirrored the emerald forest and the azure sky, now reflected a somber reality, dark and devoid of color, starkly reminiscent of Hemingway's post-war world.

However, amidst this desolate spectacle, the resilience of life began to assert itself, stubbornly clinging to hope. The lush greens and the vibrant colors were indeed gone, replaced by a stark palette of blacks, grays, and browns, but within this monochromatic landscape were faint but certain signs of life's enduring spirit.

Since that year of the Duck Lake Fire, tiny, green saplings pushed through the scorched earth, dotting the blackened terrain with spots of defiant life. Birds began to return, their warbles tentative yet hopeful, breathing a certain cadence back into the silent world. Within this devastation, the tiny saplings, the returning birds, and the determined humans painted a picture of life's resilience and the enduring hope that even in the face of desolation, life found a way.

The aftermath of the Duck Lake Fire—the sights of the charred landscape—had filled Sonny with an unspeakable sadness. But as the chill of the winter day receded and the first signs of spring came in view, Sonny decided to beach her canoe on a particularly inviting sandy slope, the hull of the canoe whispering against the fine grains in sharp contrast to the abrasive sounds of branches scraping against the canoe's sides on previous stops.

She caught sight of a young white-tailed deer cautiously emerging from the edge of the recovering forest, its curious eyes scanning the surroundings before bending to taste the tender new shoots of grass. She held her breath, a tear brimming in her eye. It was a moment of pure, unadulterated joy —a sign of hope and renewal.

Taking a cue from Armstrong's legendary words, she said, "That's one small step for Sonny, and one giant leap for Sonny kind," her voice resonating with the spirit world. She had to be careful on that ankle. After retrieving a full mountain meal from her blue barrel, she set up her pot and burner for a lazy, comforting lunch. The dune was an oasis, the sun beating down at the perfect angle to keep her warm without being overwhelming. The sand, forming a naturally ergonomic lounge chair, was more comfortable than Mitch's now neglected leather recliner back home.

Behind her shuttered eyelids, the sun's warm glow danced, weaving itself into the fabric of her dreams. Cradled in a cocoon of serene tranquility, Sonny slipped into a world painted by her subconscious—a pastel-colored canvas of her childhood home.

In the kitchen, she could almost taste the buttery richness of her mother's signature dish. It was real butter, spread generously over potatoes cooked to perfection, simmered in whole milk, and, rather than whipped violently, were mashed by hand. The tantalizing sizzle of hand-rolled Swedish meatballs seasoned meticulously, their aroma commingling with the simmering gravy, wafted through the air.

Her father was there, too, quietly positioned in the front room with his pipe and paper. She could sense his presence, a comforting certainty rooted in her childhood memories. Outside the side door, in the garage, stood the big white refrigerator, a treasure trove of her favorite drinks. They were always chilled to perfection, a blissful respite on sweltering summer days. With a satisfying pop and hiss, she opened a bottle of Faygo Orange, its metal cap joining its compatriots in the bucket below, awaiting their party.

The first gulp was a delight, an explosion of sweetness that refreshed and invigorated her, its coldness tingling down her throat. She then emerged into the backyard where beloved faces of aunts, uncles, and grandparents lounged by the pool, their smiles radiant under the sun. "You're home," they said, their voices layered with love and welcome. Each smile, each word, wrapped her in warmth and love. In this ethereal landscape, she was never alone.

Mitch was there, too. In the pool, clad in those horrendous swim trunks he was so fond of sporting every 4th of July. A drink in one hand, he bobbed gently on an inflatable, his other arm beckoning her to join. His broad smile held an invitation. "Come on in," he coaxed. "The water's great."

A foreign sound crept into her idyllic world, faint at first but rapidly growing in intensity. Was it the neighbor mowing the lawn? Perhaps a malfunctioning weed whacker or a failing car muffler? An unsettling interruption in her otherwise perfect dream.

Sonny blinked open her eyes, feeling reality seep in, its daylight puncturing the lingering haze of her dream world. A sense of tranquility cloaked her. The weight of reality gradually returned, but it wasn't unwelcome. Her heart felt full. She felt a distinct smile that had been absent in her life for so long. It had been "The Dream" again, her favorite journey back home. The vibrant memories of the place she longed for, the people she adored, warmed her from within. Mitch was there, his happiness shining through. She was home, in a place she yearned to be part of, in a perfect world she cherished in her dreams.

The noise—it was real, not a figment of her dreams. The hum wasn't a motor's drone, rather a purr—or was it a growl? The low rumble had a feral quality.

Lifting her head tentatively, her gaze caught sight of its source: an enormous cat, its head bent low at the river's edge. As if sensing her scrutiny, it lifted its head, its eyes meeting hers. A primal, guttural growl resonated from its chest, a chilling sound that was foreign to her ears.

Sonny had known fear. The thrill of haunted houses, the terror instigated by horror movies, the vertiginous dread of roller coasters, but this fear was of an entirely different, more horrifying caliber. It was the kind of fear that held her motionless, choking her voice into silence. She was alone, help nowhere near.

The bear horn strapped to her chest was her only defense. Would it work against this beast? This creature was no mere pet. Its sinewy form, blanketed in golden fur, emanated raw power. Despite the paralyzing fear, a strange urge to reach out, to touch its fur crossed her mind. It was, after all, a cat—yet its eyes spoke of an untamed wilderness, a predatory hunger. Its paws, deceptively soft, concealed lethal daggers that seemed to grow sharper by the second.

A contemplation: *Should I go for the horn?* Her hand commenced a painstakingly slow journey, inching toward her chest where the horn was fastened. She visualized it— the horn's fireplug red figure, its nozzle that needed to point away from her, the button atop it that demanded a forceful push.

The cat's growl increased in volume with each infinitesimal movement of her hand. Its muscles twitched, contracted, primed like a powerful spring about to be released. The moment was a crescendo of tension.

Her hand shot toward the horn, fumbled, missed. Desperately, she patted the area, finally grasping the metallic canister on her third attempt. Her thumb traced the groove of the button as the cat's growl reached a peak.

A yelp split the silence, sending jolts of terror ricocheting through her body. Her sweat-soaked body emitted a palpable fear that seemed to enhance the cat's awareness of her. Its nostrils flared, taking in the scent of its prey. As she freed the horn, her thumb pressed hard against the button, her other hand tremblingly pointing the nozzle at the monstrous feline. The coiled spring was released.

The horn blared, its sound piercing the stillness. It reached the cat mid-pounce. The creature's reflexes worked in Sonny's favor, twisting its trajectory in mid-air. Its full weight missed her body. Its menacing gaze held her captive, but instead of teeth ripping through flesh and claws shredding her, it landed awkwardly on her right arm, knocking the horn away, then darted over the dune, disappearing into the underbrush.

Sonny was left gasping, her heart pounding a frenzied rhythm against her chest. The sand clung to her sweat-soaked skin, a testament to her visceral fear.

Her arm was an alien, sluggish and unresponsive. The pain was a slow burn, then a sharp detonation, announcing its presence. Upon inspection, her dry suit bore the unmistakable signature of the wild cat's claws. Warmth flooded her arm, a familiar dread.

Her left hand, acting with swift efficiency, unsheathed the emergency blade from her chest and performed a hasty dissection of the sleeve below the elbow. The material parted reluctantly, revealing a spectacle of violence—punctures from the big cat's claws and a grotesque twist that her bones should not assume.

Her belongings, mockingly close, were a challenge to reach. She performed a clumsy ballet to rise without the aid of her right arm, a delicate balance of pain and determination. The dune's slope lent her aid, bringing her to her knees. "Good enough," she mumbled, a broken promise of effort.

Descending toward her canoe, she prayed to the gods of gravity and grace.

The blue barrel's lid was a stubborn adversary against her single-handed assault. Her left hand pulled and tugged, fingertips turning an alarming array of hues until, with a triumphant *POP*, the lid surrendered. She rummaged blindly until her fingers brushed against the familiar fabric of her emergency bag. The contents of the barrel cascaded into the Prospector like a waterfall of neglect.

Zippers, it seemed, were no friends to the one-handed. Through a slow dance of frustration, she managed to tease it open. She laid the half-open bag delicately on the thwart.

Sonny fumbled with the foil packets, her teeth aiding where her fingers could not. A pristine wipe emerged from its silver tomb, only to be snatched by the river. The second packet yielded under the careful guidance of teeth and left hand. The wipe was a soft whisper against her ravaged skin. She swabbed the wounds, registering the deep furrows of cut flesh. The creature had left its mark.

The cap on the vial of liquid skin offered little resistance to the efficient teamwork of teeth and left hand. She gingerly placed the vial and cap on the thwart. Her fingers, now acting as an arcade mechanical claw, clamped down on the vial's brush. As she stared at the gory tableau of her arm, she realized she was short a hand. The needle and thread option was a challenge. It was then that her gaze caught a glint of chrome—a paper binder. Salvation in the form of office supplies. Billy had indeed recommended the best equipment.

Her fingers worked with purpose, prying out the chrome handles. The binder's maw opened, capturing the straight lines of her wound. The pain was a familiar enemy, an old foe in a new battlefield. She slathered the liquid skin over the injury with a thick application like Van Gogh might layer on canvas, standing between her and certain infection. As she waited for the solution to dry, time stretched before her, elongating each second. She watched the transformation with morbid fascination, the weeping wounds quieting under the healing salve.

Unclamping the binder sent a fresh wave of pain crashing against her resolve. Yet, with determined grit, she repeated the ordeal with each claw mark, sealing her body against the hostile world.

Her medical kit offered a wealth of options—large bandages, squares of gauze, a testament to modern medical miracles. After a pause to collect her thoughts, she opted for the patches, their sterilized paper sheaths falling away under her teeth's insistence. Their use was a delicate choreography, the patches laid on the arm directly with an orbit of gauze wrapping unspooled, maintaining gentle but firm pressure on her wounds.

The flat, metal splint was in the kit as well—a prize she had crawled half a mile for days earlier for her ankle before taking the blue barrel bear wilderness adventure where

Riker had discovered it. "Blue Barrel Bear Wilderness Adventure," she repeated, a mantra to distract herself from the grim reality of her situation. "I would go on that ride if Disney opened it. Blue Barrel Bear Wilderness Adventure." The splint was going to be bad. U-shaped, it promised correction at the cost of pain. For the ankle, the splint went under the heel of the foot, providing support up the leg. For the arm, it went under the elbow, righting the arm's length to the wrist.

Searching for a stick within hands' reach yielded no results. Her gaze roved the canoe for something similar, her desperation mounting. With a burst of inspiration, she reached for the orange emergency whistle now required on every life vest. It was a flimsy ally, but it was all she had in a last resort.

Bracing herself, she bit down on the whistle and forced her arm into submission. Bone grated against bone, a symphony of agony with friction. She fought through tears for clear sight into the operation. Her splint in place, it forced her arm to follow. Sonny wrapped another layer with gauze, each revolution a promise of stability. Hiker's tape served as the final seal between the two poles, ensuring the splint would remain straight and true.

Strangely, Mitch's "forget-the-world" pills were absent from the blue barrel. Instead, Sonny took extra-strength aspirin. They went down smoothly with a swig of water.

Her heart throbbed with a bitter agony, and a pang of hurt coursed through her arm. Tender tears welled in

Sonny's eyes and began their sorrowful descent. It wasn't self-pity that provoked her suffering; no, it was genuine strife. This physical torment was simply the manifestation of a deeper, more intimate affliction—a crisis of the heart.

"Thirty years, Mitch!" Her voice echoed, reaching out toward the spectral realm. "For three long decades, I stood by your side as your wife. I provided support, remembered our special dates, guided you on the right path, nurtured our daughters, acted as your confidante and counsel. Thirty years, Mitch!"

Her voice cracked, the pain seeping into her words. "I was your unwavering ally, your constant. I stood by you until the very last breath. I gave you everything you asked for until the very last breath. But now, what is left for me? Who am I to become? I believed in us, Mitch. I thought I could do this, carry on in your absence. But I... I may not be able to. I don't know anymore, Mitch, I simply don't know."

With a sigh, she sank into the sand, exhausted from the events, the whisper of the river lulling her toward sleep. *What else will I need to survive?* she wondered, her mind teetering on the edge of consciousness.

14

In the misty landscape of her dream, Sonny looked down at herself, standing at the heart of an enormous stone labyrinth. She was draped in a threadbare robe, one arm hanging limp by her side. The stone walls around her towered menacingly, whispering of mysteries and dangers lurking in their cold shadows. With a start, she realized that the labyrinth was a manifestation of her current predicament; she was isolated, wounded, and lost.

Soon, she was not alone. A translucent, ethereal form materialized in front of her. It was Mitch, his familiar handsome face looking back at her with concern.

"Mitch," she called out, "I need you to send help."

His spectral image flickered as if caught in a gentle breeze, then steadied. "I already sent in the Marines, what more do you want?" His voice echoed, bouncing off the stone walls of the labyrinth.

"More," she called out to Mitch. "I need more!"

With a determined nod, Mitch's spectral form shimmered before fading away, leaving Sonny alone again. She felt a rush of wind and looked up just as an enormous raven descended from the sky, landing on a nearby stone. Jet black, the shaggy feathers around its throat moved with the turn of its head. The bird's long bill held something that glistened in the sun. Was it a ruby? With its head bowed, it dropped the item that fell for what seemed like an eternity until it splashed into the water below. *PLOP.* The ruby slipped beneath the surface. The world around her shook and trembled. She watched as the water below the raven's perch rose higher, spilling over the edges until the land began to flood. The water, lapping at her toes, rose quickly until she was ankle-deep. She knew that the ruby had caused this.

Sonny opened her eyes. She was still on the riverbank next to the canoe. She had fallen asleep only to wake with her arm and leg still bandaged.

Under the lingering sun, time stretched languorously, allowing for the day to unspool further. Painstakingly, and with a humility that solitude permits, she crawled to retrieve her stove, pot, and water bottle before managing to hoist herself into the waiting embrace of the canoe. She allowed herself a pause, a sweet surrender to the moment, an intimate rendezvous with her thoughts. Experimenting with the kayak paddle, she found it unwieldy, and her arm—swathed in protective skin—protested against its use. The wooden paddle gifted by Billy, however, caressed the water at an angle that promised both reach and control.

Gritting her teeth in determination, Sonny's body moved in a primal dance, pushing and pulling with her hips, until the canoe disentangled from the sandy river edge. In the river's heart, the current flirted with the canoe, twirling it around as she wrestled to control its course. Each dip of the paddle was a sweet whisper exchanged between her and the Two-Hearted, a quiet conversation of resistance and submission.

The river meandered, its path a lover's sigh between kisses, leading toward Lake Superior. The surrounding dunes, once barren, now donned a mantle of new life, the verdant aftermath of the Duck Lake Fire a decade earlier. Life's unyielding insistence on survival was on full display, sprouting seeds sprung in the wake of destruction, heralding a new beginning. The skeletal remains of the fire-kissed trees marked the passing landscape, rising and falling like the rhythm of a slumbering heart.

Fatigue tugged at Sonny, pleading with her to rest, to satiate her hunger. Ideal spots for her tent were absent, and the task of setting it up single-handedly loomed large. A hammock was an option, but the living trees were playing hard to get, too distant from one another. Resigned, Sonny decided to stay loyal to the canoe. An hour of journeying had bred familiarity; she knew she could endure, could cling to this vessel of survival.

As the sun began to flirt with the horizon, she fumbled for her flashlight and reserve, tools potent enough to pierce the impending darkness. As night's blanket began to unroll, the stars started winking down at her, celestial bodies that had once guided brave souls like Jason and his Argonauts, and explorers like Magellan, Columbus, and Vasco da Gama.

"Vasco da Gama," she murmured, finding solace in the gentle lilt of the name, whispering it into the gathering darkness.

The time seemed ripe for a touch of melody, a distraction, so she hummed "Moon River," her voice but a murmur in the wilderness. The words "Huckleberry friend" stirred memories of Johnny Mercer and a trip to Savannah, Georgia with her family. She pondered over Mercer's boyhood days picking huckleberries, his affection for Mark Twain which inspired the lyric. An owl, aroused by her song, returned a hoot that was hauntingly beautiful.

In the silence that had followed the change in landscape, Sonny became aware of the quiet symphony of the wilderness she had been a part of. The burnt terrain felt distant, while the rhythmic lullaby of Lake Superior's waves drew closer. She knew from her prior plunge that the waters of the Two-Hearted were chilly, and she expected the greatest of the Great Lakes to be more so, with icy specters of icebergs still adorning its surface this late in the season.

Her strength was ebbing, fatigue creeping in. Her thoughts meandered as she did, lazily steering the canoe to avoid the shoreline and the occasional eddy caused by a fallen cedar. Local tales whispered that the river was carved by a romantic Paul Bunyan, while others claimed it owed its name to the spirit of the place and people. Pike, Riker, and Ranger certainly proved this kindness. Looking at the map, many discerned a heart turned upside down in the split tributary. For Sonny, it would always symbolize the two hearts she shared with Mitch.

Distant voices floated toward her, surprising her. A campfire, though unseen, must be holding court to a few people, their voices reaching her at "three-beer volume" as Mitch might have termed it. As she approached a bend in the river, she noticed something reflected in the water. It was the hanging bridge near where her bike was chained, the voices from the neighboring campground.

She could halt here, declare her mission accomplished. But Sonny knew the journey wasn't over, not until the river's turbid water kissed the crystal-clear Lake Superior. Instead of turning, she watched the suspension bridge sail over her head, her flashlights catching glimpses of it. The voices from the camp grew louder as she approached, competing with the growing orchestra of waves crashing on her left.

As the towering dunes gave way to a flat beach, a celestial glow painted the horizon, the curve of the Earth dancing with the lake's lights. At the river's end, where the big Two-

Hearted sped up to merge with the lake, she steered right, the canoe coming to a halt on the beach.

With labored effort, Sonny stepped out of the canoe, her legs crying out against the cold waters and cramped hours in the Prospector. Using her one good hand and foot, she dragged the canoe onto the shore. Exhausted, she lay on top of the Prospector 14, trying to shield herself from the beach winds and potential bug bites from sand mites.

Gazing up at the starlit canvas above, her eyelids felt heavy. Just as they threatened to close with a bang, a luminescent curtain unfurled across the sky. The Northern Lights, in hues of green, purple, and red, danced to celebrate her accomplishment.

15

"What year did that incident occur?" Sonny muttered to herself, hauling the Prospector by its handle over the pebbled wash of the river. "The Blue Pontiac LeMans... must've been '70 or '71. Around the same time, they stopped making the Tempest. I was wearing that favorite cream dress of mine, didn't want it sullied. Yet, in the span of a few moments, three cars pulled over. Each man eager to lend a hand. I knew the mechanics of it all, had the jack and the spare ready, but the prospect of ruining that cream dress... So I let them. They each took turns ordering the other around, asserting their authority, while one tried to charm me. The gentleman in the blue suit, he was the one lamenting the end of the Pontiac Tempest. Ten minutes, that's all it took, and I was back on the road, each with my number stashed away to call on me later. That was way before you, Mitch."

Her progress up the shoreline to the tree line was slow and measured, each step a delicate dance, punctuated by intermittent halts.

"I wonder what's become of those three. I wouldn't mind playing the damsel now. I wonder if that's still acceptable these days. Seems like chivalry is considered an affront now. Men can't even hold the door open for a lady anymore. That's not quite true, though. Pike, Ranger, Riker—they were gentlemen, through and through."

Packing provisions into the red dry-bag, she discarded anything cumbersome and redundant. Leaving the canoe tucked away under a Jack pine off the road, her joints were protesting from the night spent curled up in the canoe. The walk up the beach stimulated circulation. She had managed a solid four-hour sleep last night, she calculated.

The slow-paced walk toward her mountain bike was surprisingly therapeutic. She observed spring rabbits gamboling in the field, their noses twitching as they nibbled. Deer, still donning their winter coats, camouflaged against the landscape, visible only when they stirred. From her position on the road, she could see remnants of winter, patches of snow in the shadowy nooks of the woods.

"Well, I really botched this one up, Mitch," she announced to the spirit world. "Should've left the truck here and taken the bike on day one. It's all backwards."

As she unlocked the bike from the tree, she noticed the "three-beer choir" had already vacated the camp. If any souls had been lingering, she might've asked for a ride back to the truck. But this was a weekday, the off-season for most, and she found herself in one of the most isolated corners of America. Wilderness preserves were designed to protect the wilderness, which meant an abundance of wildlife and a marked scarcity of humans, let alone those in vehicles.

She laid the bike flat on the ground the way she'd been taught as a child and gingerly straddled the frame, careful to protect her right foot. As she bent down, her left hand taking the brunt of the weight, the tips of her right fingers barely made contact, guiding the bike upright. When the bike started to topple, her instincts kicked in and she tried to reach out, but her right arm didn't obey. The bike took a minor bounce, but she was back up within moments.

Everything had to be done in reverse, requiring careful consideration. The additional weight from the red dry-bag on her back didn't help, shifting uneasily at the slightest motion. Placing her left foot on the raised left pedal, she pushed off slightly and bore down on the left pedal. She sent deliberate commands to her right foot, guiding it to the right pedal, then pressed down gingerly.

Riding was only marginally quicker than walking, but it was the better choice nonetheless.

She delved into her memory palace, a mental storage for mid-length memories, such as the location of her parked car, upcoming birthdays and anniversaries, and due dates for bills. She pulled forth the image of a map that hung in the Edison Room. She had taken her girls to the Henry Ford Greenfield Village every summer and adopted Edison's relocated workshop from Menlo Park, New Jersey as her personal workspace in memory. Among the maps on the wall was the one she needed for this journey: a 15-mile bike ride along routes 423, 414, and 407 back to the truck. Normally, it would be a 70-minute bike ride, but Sonny knew that today it would consume the better part of her daylight hours.

She engaged the bike's lowest gears to negotiate the uneven dirt road, skirting the sandy patches and adhering to the compacted tracks.

The first mental marker she'd stored in her Edison Room was a massive tree, bristling with directional signs at its crossroads. All 26 signs were secured to the trunk, and on this trip, she had time to count and decipher each one. The topmost sign, evidently among the oldest and weathered by the sun over many years, featured Larscoop and pointed south. Considering its height, it must have been affixed when the tree was young and crept upwards with the trunk's growth. From top to bottom, the other signs read: Camp 24, Jones, Peanut Camp, Grand Haven, Johnsons, Owl Club, Camp Buckeye, Alson, Beach Camp, East Firetower, Geoff Camp, Muskrat Inn, Elyson Club, Valhalla, East Branch Club, Camp Five, and DeFoe Camp. The last sign she read,

Popp's Camp, faded from view as she continued her slow trek.

Further down the path, she passed a hand-painted saw blade from a lumber mill. Its depiction of a sunset over water, rendered in vibrant blues, reds, and yellows, seemed to be crafted with a broad, hefty brush typically reserved for furniture or house detailing. Each tooth of the blade appeared menacingly sharp, yet was rusted enough to impart a case of tetanus. *When did I last get a tetanus shot?* she thought, pressing on at a slow, steady pace.

Exhaustion was taking its toll, but her spirits were buoyed when she spotted the Princess Bride Rock. The sight signified that the paved road was not far off, providing her a ray of hope. The continuous crunch of dirt beneath her tires served as an auditory reminder of the journey she was undertaking.

Pausing to take water at the side of 407, just off the asphalt, a silver GMC decelerated and came to a stop a few yards ahead of her. The driver disembarked and sauntered back toward Sonny.

"You need a ride," she declared, without a hint of inquiry.

"I do."

"Where to?"

"High Bridge."

"That your truck parked there?"

"It is. You know this place well?"

"I make a point of it. Name's Grace. Let's get that bike of yours." Grace's statements held an air of finality.

Grace stood a good head and a half above Sonny, her facial features strongly hinting at Scandinavian roots. Her hair was silver, and her skin bore the wear of years, revealing her age. Together, they maneuvered the bike toward the truck and hoisted it into the truck bed.

Grace, still spirited, quipped, "You been out here wrestling bears? Or that come from your man?"

"No, no, nothing like that. Just canoeing the Two-Hearted."

"Where's your canoe?"

"Other end of the river, on Superior."

Grace emitted a grunt of acknowledgment. She seemed to know her way around, driving straight to Mitch's truck at High Bridge, cutting the engine, and hopping out. When Sonny caught up, the bike had already been removed from Grace's truck bed and was waiting to be loaded onto Mitch's.

Sonny reached into her pocket and pressed the ignition button on the key fob twice, hoping to pre-warm the truck.

Together, they heaved the bike into the truck bed, Sonny guiding the front while Grace pushed the heavier part in. The bike lay flat in the truck bed and was swiftly secured with straps.

"What happened to your arm?" Grace asked.

"I'm not sure you'll believe me."

"Give it a shot."

"I think it was a cougar, or maybe a panther..."

"We got those around here. Cougars have been caught on trail cams. They roam the entire peninsula, back and forth. Seen 'em in Dollarville, by the dam, getting a drink."

"One found me. Leapt onto my arm."

"It must have been startled. They usually avoid humans."

"I woke up, and there it was."

"Sounds about right. Tell you what, I'm going to follow you to your canoe and help you get it loaded."

"That's really kind of you, thank you. I truly appreciate it."

"Us folks need to stick together up here."

"Is it that obvious?"

"Nobody around here would be bold enough to take on the Two-Hearted this early in the year. I hope you found what you were looking for."

"I hope so too."

"Let's get going. The cab should be warmed up by now." Grace patted the truck twice before returning to her vehicle.

Their twin trucks trundled past a sign announcing "Authorized Vehicles Only." Grace reassured her, "Don't worry, sister. You're authorized" when Sonny had hesitated initially. The road she'd trodden that morning suddenly felt insignificant in the truck. What had been a near thirty-minute walk was under a minute's drive, highlighting the extent of her injury.

Sonny shared this with Grace, to which she replied, "Isn't that what we always tell ourselves? It will be different for us."

"Yeah. Yeah, that's right."

"Tell me about something you did recently."

They ambled side by side toward the canoe.

"Well, I canoed the Two-Hearted."

"And everyone warned you that it's dangerous, reckless even. And what did you tell yourself? That I'm different. That I wouldn't get hurt."

"It was just a canoe trip, like the ones from scouts."

"Exactly. Grab that end." Grace took the weightier end laden with gear by the handle, murmuring low enough for Sonny to hear, "Nice canoe."

One on each end, they hauled the Prospector 14 back to Mitch's truck bed.

"That's the tricky thing in life," Grace said. "Coming to terms with being human. Sure, you're unique in some ways, but not really. You're just like everyone else."

"I thought the lesson was to get back up, to keep going."

"Nah, that's kids' stuff. The real lesson? You do the best you can, improve a little every day. You'll stumble. Just like everyone else. Because you *are* everyone else."

As they set the canoe down at the edge of the truck, Sonny began loading everything into the blue barrel that would fit. Then, every item—the blue barrel, red dry-bag, wooden paddle, kayak paddle, medical kit—found a place in the back of the cab.

Hoisting the canoe's bow into the bed of Mitch's truck,

Sonny retorted, "I canoed the big Two-Hearted in early spring. That makes me different, not like everyone else."

Assisting with pushing the canoe further into the bed, Grace replied, "You survived. That's what makes you different." Grace heaved the stern as Sonny closed the truck bed gate with a resounding slam.

"I survived."

"Yep." Grace flashed a crooked smile. "I'll tail you into Newberry, get you to the health center for that arm."

"You've already done so much."

"I'm following you into town. You're going to the clinic." It was a statement, not a question.

"Sounds good."

As they merged onto 500 South from 414, the satellite radio sprung back to life. Sonny assumed her phone was also back in service. She followed her earlier route in reverse: 500 turned from dirt road to pavement as it merged into 123, leading her into Newberry, the heart of the Tahquamenon River Valley. *What will I tell the girls?* she asked herself.

16
───────

Sonny followed the blue sign with the silver "H" that marked the entrance to Helen Newberry Joy Hospital & Healthcare Center. The substantial building appeared to serve all of Luce County.

The attending receptionist's face said it all as Sonny limped in. She reeked—a potent blend of Lake Superior, river water, the aftermath of relieving herself against a tree, body odor, and fear, along with other, more indefinable scents from the journey. "I need you to fill this paperwork out. Make sure to include your full name, date of birth, and your reason for visiting us today," the attendant instructed.

Living in a world turned upside down, Sonny attempted to pen her information with her left hand. Her scrawl was nearly legible—perhaps she was suited to be a doctor from this evidence.

A few minutes later, Grace entered with a man dressed in a brown uniform. They took seats on either side of Sonny. "This is my friend Rick," Grace began. "He's in charge of the DNR here in Luce County. I told him about your cougar."

"Ma'am."

"Hold on, your name is Rick? And you're a DNR ranger?"

"That's correct, ma'am. I get the joke."

"Ranger Rick, how can I assist?" Sonny couldn't help but smile at the absurdity of it all. In the scheme of the week's events, this was certainly a lighter moment. "I'm sorry, your name's not funny. It's just... this week has been... I—"

Rick pulled a map from his jacket and unfolded it. "Could you point out where you were attacked?"

"I wish I'd had this map with me earlier. Look at the details. It shows the terrain and everything."

"We provide these at the station. All you need to do is drop by and check-in before heading out into the woods."

"I was around here," she said, pointing. "The fire line had passed, and I was on a large dune. I fell asleep in the sun. When I woke, it was there, drinking from the river."

"I see. In the burn area, interesting."

"I used the bear horn, scared it off, but it pounced—it was just like an oversized, furious house cat."

"This one could rip your arm off."

"Well, besides that."

"What color was it?"

"Orange brown-ish."

"Goldie Hawn."

"I'm sorry, it has a name?"

"Goldie Hawn is the golden one; her black companion is Kurt Russell." Grace elaborated, "They've been around for a few years now. Hard not to name them."

"Goldie's spotted more often, due to her color. Kurt Russell is stealthier, harder to spot in the forest," Rick explained.

"Do you think they'll have kittens this year?" Grace inquired.

"She should be old enough to have cubs soon," Rick answered before turning to Sonny. "Did you see a red tag on her ear?"

Sonny closed her eyes, attempting to recall. "I don't know, I—I can't—maybe?"

"Sonny?" the attendant called. "The doctor will see you now."

As the attendant beckoned her, a nurse appeared from a hallway with a wheelchair, assisting her into it. He pushed her down a hall, clicked the wheel locks into place, and told her, "I'll be right back." True to his word, he returned a minute later, leading her into a room with eight beds, separated by white fabric partitions on a track in the ceiling. He helped her stand and remove her hiking pants. In the stark, real-world lighting, Sonny was taken aback by the sight of her legs. The colorful array of bruises resembled the topographical markings on Ranger Rick's map.

"Welp, you don't see that kind of coloring on a leg every day," he declared. He made quick work of the bandages she'd fashioned in the wilderness, revealing an ankle grotesquely swollen. "The doctor will be here soon. There's no cause for concern."

His manners were agreeable, his touch light as he began to work on her arm. As he endeavored to cut through the hiking tape, unraveling the layers of makeshift bandage that held her arm rigid, the scissors became lodged. When the layers of the handmade cocoon finally peeled away, it revealed what looked like Goya's Saturn with all the dark colors of bruised skin, the bend where the break happened, and three distinct gashes from the cat claw.

"What's this, here? Some sort of adhesive? Super glue?" he queried.

"Liquid skin," she replied.

He grunted, moving to a computer, fingers dancing across the keys.

"Sonny, I am Doctor Drake," the woman walking in introduced herself. "I understand you've had a rather eventful week. Care to share?"

Sonny paused, knowing full well her tale would sound ludicrous. "Would it be alright to take a few photos before we start?"

"Photos?"

"No one is going to believe my tale, not without some proof."

The nurse took three photos of her arm, three of her leg. While he was busy, Sonny told Doctor Drake about dropping in at High Bridge, tripping on the trail, and waking up to Goldie Hawn.

"You've met Rick, then?"

"I have."

"He does take pride in his names."

Following the cleanup, Drake called for X-rays. The medical center was small, nothing like the bustling places where Sonny had spent years with Mitch, a revolving door of strangers witnessing intimate moments of struggle and vulnerability. Here, it was just Doctor Drake and the nurse. They took the X-ray images, pored over them in a separate room, and then wheeled Sonny to a private room. They cleaned her arm once more and washed down her leg.

Drake decided against a hard cast. The lacerations on her arm necessitated a soft cast, one that could be easily removed for regular inspections. There was bad news, too.

The rebreaking and resetting of her arm was a kind of pain she'd never known, like a vicious explosion of agony. Nearest so far to giving birth to the twins. Of all the suffering that week, this was the whopper. Though the liquid skin had worked as intended, it was replaced by stitches. Painful, but nothing compared to the brute force of Goldie Hawn or the hand-mine that reached out and ensnared her ankle on the trail.

Once the procedures were done, Drake allowed her a few

minutes to recover. "You're lucky to be alive, Sonny," she said. "What you did was remarkable. But don't do it again."

Grace peeked in. "Yeah, the admin wants the paperwork filled out again, I figure you might be right-handed. Why don't we do this together?"

17

The seat warmer hummed into life, soothing Sonny's tired body. She flicked a glance at the dashboard clock. 8:15. *Now or never*, she thought, thumbing the cell phone to dial Glinda's number.

"Hello?"

"Glinda, it's Mom. I'm looping in your sister, sit tight."

With practiced ease, she activated the three-way call feature, dialing Evanora.

"Mom?"

"Hold on." One click later, she resumed, "Don't freak out."

Evanora scoffed, "Too late."

Sonny sighed. "Alright, fine. I'm okay."

"Now I really don't believe you," Evanora snarked.

"I knew this would backfire," Sonny muttered.

"Spit it out, Mom." Glinda intervened.

"To cut to the chase, my arm's broken and my ankle's twisted."

"We'll come to get you," Glinda immediately offered.

"No need, I'm in the hospital lot, got my arm set, ankle braced. And I can drive."

Evanora cut in, "Hold on. That's a load of bull. Your driving's compromised."

"I can handle it," Sonny assured.

Glinda's voice softened. "Mom, don't push it tonight. Get a room, sleep it off. We'll talk in the morning."

"Alright."

Evanora chimed in, "Yes, listen to Glinda. Do not, I repeat, *do not* drive."

"Mom." Glinda paused. "Evanora and I, we're worried. We care about you. There's this thing called the widow effect. People tend to—"

"Jesus, Glinda!" Evanora interjected, "Way to break it to her gently! Are you reading off a script?"

"It's also known as 'broken heart syndrome' or 'takotsubo cardiomyopathy..'"

"Christ, she's got notes!" Evanora groaned. "Mom, don't mind Glinda. But we are worried. Call us if you need anything..."

"Yes, Mom, grief heals with time."

"Glinda, for crying out loud, shut up!"

"Girls—"

"Unbelievable! You had to go there."

"Girls."

They fell silent.

"Girls." Sonny sighed. "I won't be home as planned, but I'm okay. That's it."

"Check in later, Mom," Glinda requested.

"Yeah, call us."

"Goodnight, girls." Sonny cut the call, reclining in her seat, alone in the dimly lit parking lot.

Decisions didn't always need to be tough. The choice between truck slumber and a cozy hotel room? Simple. Unfortunately, the painkillers Doctor Drake had given her were hardly more potent than aspirin. It was a pain that gnawed, promising to keep sleep at bay until sheer exhaustion forced surrender.

Sonny spent the next hour and a half driving southeast, the Mackinac Bridge emerging in her path. Crossing it, she spotted a welcoming beacon of a hotel sign, "Vacancy" glowing brightly against the night. Sixty-five dollars awarded her a comfortable room and a splendid view of the illuminated bridge, a spectacle of red, white, and blue lights dancing on the water below. The faint rumble of truck engines employing their brakes to negotiate the bridge's descent was distant, more a lullaby than a disturbance.

Her ankle, it seemed, had taken the drive in stride, its protests subtle. There had been a moment, a flash of tawny fur, wide eyes reflecting headlight beams when she'd doubted her reflexes. The deer, however, had more sense, retreating just as swiftly as it had appeared.

One part of Sonny longed for "The Dream," the delicious warmth that came from being enveloped in the presence of her loved ones. Yet another part dreaded sleep, fearing a return to that desolate labyrinth of loneliness. Why would Mitch send her a raven in that dream?

She was supposed to live out the next few decades of her life alongside Mitch, her eternal love. But instead, she was grappling with the dawn of each day on her own. As she drove, her mind wandered back to the qualities that had drawn her to Mitch in the first place. Among many things, it was his thoughtful planning that had captivated her. He saw her as someone deserving of a meticulously crafted world, a world built on thoughtfulness and care for them to navigate together. Her prior boyfriends, on the other hand, had been nothing more than fleeting allies. They seemed intriguing at the outset, but their self-centeredness surfaced sooner than later.

It might seem old-school to see Mitch as a provider, but that's what he was and more. He valued Sonny not as a passing amusement, but as someone not to be taken lightly. Her past suitors reveled in the pursuit, but once they had her, they didn't know what to do. What would her dating life look like now? It was unrealistic to expect the high standard of Mitch, but was it too much to hope for someone who could at least come halfway?

They wouldn't have the same idiosyncrasies or shared memories. Did she have the patience or the inclination to train a new man? No, that wasn't quite right. Did she possess the patience and curiosity to spend that much time understanding a new individual? Many people she met seemed fickle and artificial. All she wanted was a reasonably attractive man who she could connect with and spend at least four hours a day with. Was that ask unachievable?

18

Dorothy's first inquiry about Oz was straightforward: "Is he a good man?" The response, arriving directly from Oz himself two-thirds of the way through the novel, was confessional: "I am a good man, but a bad wizard." Dorothy offered her own self-definition, "I'm just an ordinary girl from a strange land." As the miles passed on her homeward journey, with Mitch's truck dutifully sharing the labor of driving, Sonny's mind strayed to the pages of L. Frank Baum's tale for children. A tale she had cherished since her own girlhood, and which she had read to the twins as they grew, until memorized, the words becoming part of their shared childhood vernacular.

Her initial encounter with Mitch was wrapped in that memory, her asking of him that same question, "Is he a good man?" Mitch, in his way, mirrored Oz, a good man without a claim to wizardry, yet he wove an enchantment into her life just the same. Now Mitch had journeyed to that "undiscovered country," leaving her to wander, a stranger in this now unfamiliar world.

In the quiet of her arrival home, she sat in the truck, its lights extinguished, for a lengthy twenty minutes before marshaling the bravery to descend. Her left leg, stronger, facilitated her exit more easily than her entry. She had to twist her body awkwardly, relying on her left hand for balance as she carefully stepped down. There was no urgency. No expectant faces waiting inside for her. She anticipated a house as she left it, littered with untouched possessions she didn't really need. The encroaching darkness was soon to arrive. With methodical movements, the red dry-bag found its home in the garage, followed by the blue barrel, and the mountain bike resumed its usual place. A solution for the Prospector remained elusive, and it was left for the night in the bed of the truck. With her left arm aching from overuse and her right arm flinching with pain from moving the bike, she deemed the job done. Her gaze lifted to the sky before she entered the house. It was the same expanse, albeit with fewer twinkling stars. The trees in her yard stood as familiar sentinels, yet she was acutely aware of the neighbors, unseen but present, just beyond the fence. Alone, she faced this world, sobered by the depth of her loneliness.

The sting of Grace's words bore into her, an unwelcome tenant occupying her thoughts without paying rent. Sonny had long known she wasn't extraordinary, but for years, she had been the star in someone's universe. Not a superhero, not Wonder Woman for the masses, but a marvel in his world. That realization served only to deepen her melancholy. Sonny was ordinary. When it came to societal statistics, she fell squarely in the majority. A suburban house, marriage, two kids, two cars, middle-class with some savings tucked away—Sonny was the very epitome of average.

Inside the sanctuary of her home, she sank into the chair at her computer desk, intent on substantiating the insinuations Grace had tossed so casually into their conversation. Life expectancy had indeed risen, now pegged at 78 years. A growing number of those over 65 lived in solitude—another tick on the list. Heart disease and cancer continued to reign as the leading agents of mortality. The data she unearthed only echoed her own somber sentiments, etching them deeper into the fabric of her reality.

Such a happy way to end her day, she went to bed.

THE MORNING BROUGHT with it the scent of coffee and a modest breakfast, but more importantly, it brought clarity and sunlight to aid in her unpacking. Mitch's old workbench served as her platform, on which she meticulously sorted and cleaned each item from the red dry-bag and blue barrel. The hammock was hung out to air dry, and each vessel was vacuumed and wiped down, an effort to stave off mold and decay. She found an empty plastic tub, which would serve as their long-term storage.

Every item she laid hands on triggered a recollection, a fragment of the adventure they had shared. The overnight halt on the peninsula, the way it had been discarded by the bear after its brief fascination had waned, the way it had borne her down the river, over fallen trees, and across land during portage. Each memory was a testament to her resourcefulness, to the fitness of her body that made these adventures possible.

The gloom of the previous night was eradicated with the final grains of sand that she shook from the Prospector 14. She resolved to cling to these memories, to the adventure that made her feel like Wonder Woman, where she had accomplished feats of amazement. Surely, if any average person could achieve these things, the task would be simple and the Two-Hearted River would be teeming with tourists. But it wasn't, and that was a testament to her strength and endurance.

Sonny found a fiery determination to make the most of this day. The whiteboard on the kitchen refrigerator, once the home of shared grocery lists, was wiped clean of past requests—now irrelevant as her only need was to buy what she desired.

Her new list was straightforward:

1) Clean house, discard, donate. The subsequent steps

were pragmatic: Hire a removal service. Schedule a pickup with Goodwill. Notify the girls to pick what they want.

2) Sell the house. This included: Identify a trustworthy real estate agent. Prepare the house for viewing.

3) Find a new home. Beneath this, she added a few options with corresponding question marks: Apartment? Townhouse? City?

A new beginning was clearly on her horizon.

Initiating a conference call with her twins, Sonny steeled herself for what she knew was going to be a challenging conversation. "I'm okay, girls. Made it back yesterday."

"That's wonderful, Mom," Glinda responded with relief.

"That's a relief, Mom. Can we come by to see you?" Evanora asked with concern.

"Of course. But there's a new house rule," Sonny declared.

"Oh dear, what's this about?" Evanora was curious.

"Each time you visit, you're required to leave with at least five items."

"What?" Evanora exclaimed, baffled.

"I'm planning to sell the house. So, if there's anything you want, you need to start taking it. If there are disputes, you'll have to settle them between yourselves—"

"I want Grandma's gold clock," Glinda cut her off.

"I want the China set," Evanora countered.

"The Afghan! I get the Afghan," Glinda shot back.

"The pendant. I want the pendant," Evanora insisted.

"Girls, it sounds like—" Sonny attempted to intervene.

"Dad's desk," Evanora said, staking her claim.

"Shit. Dad's first-edition, signed copy of *The Old Man and The Sea*, then," Glinda retaliated.

"No. Enough. Stop," Sonny commanded. "No one gets the Hemingway; that's mine. You take five items minimum each visit. If you've already made a list, which you apparently have, you can sort it out. I don't need to referee."

"Can I call dibs on the house?" Evanora asked.

"Pretty sneaky, sis."

"You can make a reasonable offer. I am selling the house and the minivan. Also, I'm starting to clean today. A week from now, Goodwill will pick up the rest, and I've hired someone to remove what's left."

"Mom, that's really fast. What's your next move? What's the plan?" Evanora queried.

"I'm not sure yet. But it's happening soon. You better brace yourselves."

"Can we do this next week? This week is kinda full," Glinda requested.

"If you want anything, you'll make the time," Sonny concluded firmly.

19

"Just one meeting, Mom, that's all I ask. Will that really be the end of the world?" Glinda implored.

"I just don't see the point. They'll spend the whole time talking about themselves, and I won't connect with any of it," Sonny argued, pausing momentarily. "It will just be a waste of time."

"And what else are you doing?" Glinda challenged.

"Packing, cleaning, planning," Sonny retorted.

"Just one hour, Mom. That's all I ask," Glinda pleaded.

"All right, all right. I'll do it," Sonny finally capitulated. "But wait, before you go."

"Yes, Mom?" Glinda's voice changed pitch as if anticipating a heartfelt "thank you" or "I love you" as a token of her mother's appreciation for her efforts.

"You've only taken four items. The rule is five. You need to take one more thing before you leave," Sonny reminded.

"Oh, right, okay, Mom," Glinda responded, glancing at the small items on the entryway table. "I'll take this bowl."

"Drive safe. And next time, bring an empty car to load up," Sonny instructed. "Evanora, are you almost done? Have you gathered your five items for this visit?" she questioned.

"Mom," Evanora called, joining her mother and sister in the entryway. "Who is this in the photo?"

"Where did you find that?" Sonny's voice tightened.

"It was behind Dad's photo in the frame from his study." Evanora held up the folded photo that revealed an unfamiliar woman when unfurled. "Who is she?"

For a moment, Sonny looked cornered, but then her voice came out swift, like she was pulling off a bandage. "That's your father's first wife."

Evanora's jaw hit the floor.

"I'm sorry, I must have heard wrong. Did you say, 'your father's first wife'?" Glinda sounded incredulous.

"That's exactly what I said. Your father was married when we first met," Sonny stated plainly.

"But what about the literary club you met at? The story about your heart melting and knowing he was 'the one'?" Evanora questioned.

"All true," Sonny confirmed, her eyes distant. "I just didn't tell you about Lillith Worner." The name came out of her mouth like a bitter taste. "She was from Indiana. They met in college, I think."

"Mom, the date on this photo can't be right. You said you were 28 when you met Dad," Evanora interjected, her eyebrows furrowing.

"That's correct. Now, do you girls have all your things? At least five items?" Sonny tried to divert their attention.

"If that's the case, Mom, Dad was twelve years older than you," Evanora calculated, her eyes narrowing.

Sonny exhaled deeply. "Took you this long to do the math?"

"Mom," Evanora defended herself. "This just casts a new light on our lives."

"I knew you were younger, Mom, but twelve years? You made it seem like two," Glinda chimed in.

"Two, ten, what does it matter? We were in love," Sonny insisted.

"But you were the other woman," Evanora pointed out painfully. "You would never have approved that for us."

"I was another woman, not the other woman," Sonny corrected.

"I need to think about this," Glinda stammered, making a hasty exit. Her four items teetered precariously in her arms, the bowl looking ready to tumble off the top.

"Well..." Sonny began.

"Don't. My sister and I are in agreement on this," Evanora cut her off, heading for the door. "I don't know what to say."

Sonny stood in the entrance, listening to the sounds of car doors opening and closing; engines starting then fading into the distance. Alone again, surrounded by boxes she'd spent days packing, her mind wandered back to the day she met Mitch at the book club. It was the most charming of meet-cutes; he had accidentally spilled coffee on her blouse. He was so apologetic and insistent on helping her clean it up. She hadn't known he was married then. She only saw his kind eyes, his strong chin, and his gentle demeanor. His interactions with Lillith made them seem more like siblings or cousins, not a wedded couple. Sure, they shared some interests, but it was with Mitch that Sonny had discovered shared values. Lillith had always struck her as more of a free spirit with radical ideas for the era, which Mitch didn't seem to fully endorse. Sonny had never expressed it explicitly, but she had always gotten the impression that Mitch felt trapped in that relationship.

But how to explain that to the twins?

"Mom?" Evanora switched on the garage light. "Is that you? What are you doing in my garage at two in the morning?"

Emerging sheepishly from behind the crossover, Sonny replied, "Yes, it's me."

"Couldn't this have waited until morning?"

"I had a box of your things from your old room. I thought I'd save you a trip," Sonny explained.

"You thought you'd stow it away on my garage shelf in the middle of the night? It looks like there are two boxes, not one."

"Two," Sonny corrected herself. "I meant two."

"Mom, you're leaving emotional landmines everywhere. You're being an emotional terrorist."

"It's been days since either you or Glinda have been by, and I need to prep the house for the real estate agent and her photographer."

Evanora shook her head in disbelief. "You're so different, and it isn't just about Dad. Why are you rushing this? Why won't you attend a group session with the grief counselor?"

"Pastor John? No, thank you. He'll want to pray, and the others will get too chatty. I'm not interested. It didn't work for me when your father was alive. Drinking bad coffee in the hospital's function room with strangers... hearing all the stories... it's merely a distraction, not genuine help."

"Where are you rushing to, Mom?" Evanora asked.

"Rushing?"

"You ran off to the north woods thinking you could escape your problems, and you nearly killed yourself. Weeks later, you're still limping, dragging that cane everywhere, and your arm is encased in that inflatable swim toy. You need to recover."

"It's a prescribed air cast," Sonny clarified.

"Fine."

"I nearly lost my arm."

"I've seen the pictures," Evanora acknowledged.

Sonny glanced at her injured arm. "It's healing. The doctor said Goldie Hawn missed the tendon. My muscles are getting stronger."

"Didn't he also instruct you to take it easy?" Evanora queried.

"Her exact words were 'exercise caution.'" A note of optimism crept into Sonny's voice. "On a brighter note, next week I get a hard cast and the stitches come out."

"Great, Mom." Evanora sounded drained. "What's next? Why are you in such a rush?"

"I... I can't say, honey."

Tired and exasperated, Evanora flicked off the light. "Goodnight, Mom. No more boxes. Please, just donate the rest. We're all full up on crazy here, thank you."

Left standing in the dark garage, Sonny was uncertain of her next move. She considered placing the second box on the shelf next to the first but decided against it, leaving it on the garage floor.

Sonny made her way back to the truck, where two more boxes destined for Glinda's garage awaited delivery.

20

"Mother!" Evanora's voice echoed. "Mother?" She moved cautiously, threading her way through the maze of boxes cluttering the hallways. "The door was open, so I..." Evanora halted in the kitchen doorway. "Apologies, am I intruding?"

Perched atop the kitchen island, Sonny sat cross-legged, beer in hand, resembling a nightclub chanteuse serenading her audience from atop a grand piano. Her audience, however, was a trio of young men—one alarmingly tall, another highly proficient, but all muscular and undeniably attractive.

"Not at all, dear," Sonny responded. "We're merely pausing from loading the truck. Evanora, meet Ranger, Riker, and Pike. Gentlemen, this is Evanora, one of my daughters."

"Sonny, you neglected to mention your daughter's striking beauty," Pike interjected, offering his right hand to Evanora. His devilish grin widened. "A pleasure."

Matching his smile, Evanora responded, "A pleasure to meet you as well. How did you become acquainted with my mother?"

"They're my rescuers from the Two-Hearted," Sonny elaborated. "These are the Marines who saved my life."

The tallest of the three cleared his throat.

"My apologies, Ranger." Sonny swiftly corrected herself, "The soldiers who saved my life."

Evanora beamed. "It's an honor to meet you all. Thank you for saving my mother."

"Well, we didn't exactly do much," Riker admitted. "By the time we found her, she had already patched herself up. We merely ensured her safety for a while."

"Thank you," Evanora repeated.

Sonny grinned. "You'll find yourself expressing that sentiment often around these three. 'Thank you' seems to be their favorite refrain. I say it to them all the time." She extended her hand to Ranger, who gallantly helped her down from the counter. "Thank you."

"Boys," Pike initiated, "let's finish with the hallway boxes and we should be all set."

They offered Evanora warm smiles as they moved past her into the hallway. The slight ruckus of their movement was quickly replaced with the first drawn-out notes of a familiar tune—"Heigh-ho... Heigh-ho..."—before the door clicked shut behind them. The melody continued, growing fainter as they headed toward the front yard.

Evanora turned to Sonny, confusion evident in her eyes.

"In short, they affectionately refer to me as Snow White and see themselves as my loyal dwarfs," Sonny elucidated.

"They're certainly young and handsome. You must enjoy the attention."

"It's rather agreeable, Evanora. Not unpleasant at all."

Evanora moved to a cupboard to retrieve a glass, finding it disappointingly empty. She glanced at her mother, questioning.

"Sold them all at the garage sales," Sonny informed. "Would you like a beer?"

"No, thank you. I'm driving," Evanora declined, disappointed. "Your friends were very kind to help with the move."

"They're good souls. I'm fortunate to have crossed paths with them."

"It's a little melancholy, seeing you nearly done moving out. I missed all the commotion."

"There wasn't much excitement, to be honest," Sonny explained. "Everything that wasn't sold in the garage sales, donated, or given away is heading to storage."

"What remains?" Evanora inquired, leaning on the kitchen island.

"The books, some clothing, a few mementos of your father."

"I miss him."

"I've missed the man he was for the past two years," Sonny confessed. "He changed."

"It's a shame you're selling the house."

"The thing is, Evee, it's just a house," Sonny attempted to comfort her. "It was a home when your father and sister were here. You have a home. It's just not here anymore; it's with your husband and children. This is a house. And it's far too large for me, alone."

"And what's next for you? Do you have a place to stay?"

"Well..." Sonny hesitated. "The boys and I are going on a trip."

"Really?"

"Yes, we're departing for France next week."

"France?"

"We're embarking on the Camino de Santiago, the pilgrimage of St. James. It begins in France, continues through Spain, and ends in the city of Santiago de Compostela."

"And where is that?"

"On the Atlantic coast of the Iberian Peninsula."

"That's quite the journey. Is this another one of your Hemingway-inspired adventures you and Dad planned?"

"Not exactly, although Hemingway did travel parts of the

route. This is a personal venture, one I discovered through my three new friends."

"I don't understand, mother." Evanora's frustration began to show. "You're evading something. I can see it. Something's happened, or is happening, that you're not sharing. Something, I don't know, significant, perhaps trivial, but definitely something."

"Evanora, I think you're still reeling from your father's—"

"No, it's something else. You're not denying it."

"What if there *was* something, Evanora? A secret between Mitch and me that we chose not to share with you? Would you let it be if that were the case? If you knew that?"

"Well, I don't know."

"You keep secrets too. You don't share everything. Can't your dear, old mother do the same?"

"I suppose. It's just... it feels different. More substantial. You would tell me if it were something like that."

"When have I ever kept secrets from you, my dear?" Sonny approached her daughter for an embrace.

Evanora relished the warmth, the comforting knowledge of a mother's love and enduring presence. For a fleeting moment, she pondered how anyone without a mother managed to navigate life. Then, pulling away, she objected, "Wait. My entire life. That business about Dad's first wife. Your age, his age... you both lied."

"We were protecting you, Evanora," Sonny defended.

"That's all. Parents desire nothing more than to safeguard their children."

Evanora's face reflected her lingering doubts. The sound of boxes being hefted and the echoing chorus of "It's off to work we go" resonated from the hall. Evanora studied her mother from head to toe. "I don't know you. You're not who I believed you to be."

"Evanora," Sonny pleaded. "Don't leave like this. Please, Evanora."

21

The day was radiant with the signature Spanish sun as it cast a benevolent gaze upon Sonny. They'd made a decision to indulge, choosing to luxuriate within the comforts of a hotel room in Pamplona after journeying an additional three days to the city. Their wandering spirits guided them through the sacred halls of the Church of San Saturnino, along the infamous route of the bull run leading to Plaza de Toros, and finally to the heart of Pamplona: Plaza del Castillo, where they paused for a refreshing cerveza.

"I adore these chilled Mahou," Sonny professed, an expression of her love she'd repeated to the point of charming monotony.

"We're well aware," responded her towering friend with a fond grin.

A gentle zephyr swept across the plaza, tenderly cooling the band of travelers beneath the cerulean canvas adorned with fluffy white clouds. Sonny was submerged in a dream come true, basking in a sense of belonging, autonomy, deep-rooted friendships, and the satisfaction of daily accomplishments. An unparalleled sense of wholeness suffused her.

"That mountain ascent from France to cross the border, I was unsure if we'd make it," Sonny confessed to her trio. "But we made it. The challenges are mere memories. Spain has been a divine delight."

Riker, raising his glass in anticipation of a toast, suggested, "Cin-Cin."

Sonny savored the ice-cold Mahou as it danced on her tongue and glided down her throat. From the corner of her eye, she watched Riker relish his beloved brew. She couldn't help but imagine his strong arms around her. She studied the muscles in his forearms as they moved, curiosity swirling within her at the thought of such raw power pulling her close, pressing against her. With a mere hint or suggestion, she could envision herself surrendering to his will.

"After this one, I plan to indulge in a siesta," Sonny confessed.

As the sun began its descent, the heat, intensified by light, was shielded by her sunglasses.

"I could do with a nap," Pike proposed. "Does that make me lazy?"

"It's not the desire; it's evidence of your laziness," Ranger rejoined.

The quartet ambled their way toward the Hotel Tres Reyes, their steps steady and sure on stones that bore the weight of centuries and countless visitors. Their jovial camaraderie made the journey to their rooms a celebration, a respite from the sun's persistent heat.

Three hours into slumber, Sonny's phone buzzed against the bedside table. Its vibration rattled the tranquility, forcing her into wakefulness. Her mind lingered in the realm of dreams, where she felt nothing but warmth and love, trust and happiness.

"Hello?" she answered, her voice still laced with sleep and the effects of many Mahou.

"Hello, Mom," Glinda's voice came, its familiar, pleasant tone acting like a charm.

"Glinda, how are you? I am so happy to hear your voice."

"I'm well, Mom, but I'm worried about Evanora. She's distressed, feeling ostracized. She said it's as if a house has been dropped on her. Could you perhaps give her a call?"

Sonny sighed. "She won't take my calls, Glinda. I try every week, but it goes straight to voicemail. What do you call that?"

"Ghosting?"

"Yes, ghosting. That's exactly what she's doing."

"Mom, have you been drinking?"

"A little, there's this splendid beer here, Mahou. I've been having tastes most of the day."

"I'm glad you're enjoying yourself. But I'm still concerned about Evanora. She believes you're concealing something."

"I wouldn't know where to begin, Glinda. I've been feeling guilty."

"You always said it's always best to start at the beginning."

"Glinda... I just... it's... you two might stop speaking to me if I tell you."

Her daughter's voice was gentle, yet insistent. "It will take you home in just two seconds. You can tell me."

Sonny confessed, her voice barely a whisper, "I was weak. After nearly two years, I couldn't bear it anymore. I had a moment of weakness."

"Did you cheat on Dad? He would understand."

"No, no, nothing of the sort. I loved your father deeply. We fit together so perfectly. But it was never-ending. He kept asking for things. I couldn't sleep. The only person I saw was the grocery delivery man. I had no one to confide in."

"What happened, Mom?"

"He kept wanting me to carry him to his truck, but he was too heavy. He talked about Hemingway in that last year, after the plane crash." Sonny turned in her bed, her hair disheveled, head spinning. "I was weak. I gave in. I did what he asked. I took his pillow, placed it over him, and pressed. Fuck, it took an eternity. He couldn't struggle. Once I started, there was no end but to end it."

Her voice cracked, tears spilling forth. "I was weak. I didn't stop, Glinda. Don't tell Evanora. Please, don't say anything. She wouldn't understand. Glinda? Glinda?"

SONNY STIRRED, her mind heavy with sleep, disoriented as she tried to grasp where she was. The deep slumber had taken its toll, clouding her memory. Then it all came back to her. She was a pilgrim, an ordinary girl in an extraordinary land, journeying with her closest companions in search of the answers to life. Was this a dream? Where did reality end and dreams begin?

As she bathed under the soothing spray of hot water, she let the day's stress drain away. "Breathe," she whispered to herself. "Just breathe and take the next day as it comes."

She took time to primp for the evening. The more she looked into the mirror, the better she felt about herself. She saw herself reflected back as a good person. She could look herself in the eyes and believe that she was a good person.

Descending the hotel's central staircase, she found Riker comfortably ensconced in the lobby, engrossed in a copy of *East of Eden* she lent.

"What do you think?" Sonny asked.

He turned to a dog-eared page he'd marked. "I believe a strong woman may be stronger than a man, particularly if she happens to have love in her heart. I guess a loving woman is indestructible." He closed the book, a knowing smile on his face. "I see why you like this one. You ready to meet up with the boys? They're saving us a spot."

"I'm famished. Let's get lost."

ABOUT THE AUTHOR

Paul Michael Peters is a story-
teller with an original voice who
thrives at the edge of the human
condition, blending humor and
darkness with keen insight. His
tales navigate the intricate dance
between the mundane and the
profound, capturing the
ephemeral moments that define
our lives with passion. His work
invites readers into a world
where the ordinary becomes extraordinary, exploring life's
shadowy corners with narratives that resonate with authen-
ticity and imaginative daring.

Dive into the work of Paul Michael Peters and discover
stories that echo the complexities of life: "Broken Objects,"
"Combustible Punch," "The Symmetry of Snowflakes,"
"Insensible Loss," and several beloved short stories like "Mr.

Memory and Other Stories of Wonder." Find free chapter previews at paulmichaelpeters.com.

Follow him at:
Website: https://www.paulmichaelpeters.com/

If you enjoyed this book, please consider leaving a positive review on one of these websites:

Bookbub: https://www.bookbub.com/authors/paul-michael-peters

Goodreads: https://www.goodreads.com/author/show/7077098.Paul_Michael_Peters

ALSO BY PAUL MICHAEL PETERS

RIGHT HAND OF THE RESISTANCE

In a world eerily parallel to our own, life is bisected by the Barrier—
a monolithic edifice that symbolizes division and control. It
segregates nations and dictates the very fate of those bold enough to
cross. "Right Hand of the Resistance" by Paul Michael Peters melds
the heart-pounding suspense of Tom Clancy, the speculative genius
of Dan Simmons, and the prescient vision of George Orwell to
capture the essence of a divided society. It challenges the Golden
Rule by asking, "How well should we treat one another?" The

narrative follows perilous treks to the north, fraught with danger yet illuminated by the hope of a better existence beyond the oppressive divide.

Paul Michael Peters maps a world where passage across the Barrier involves high costs and profound sacrifices, all under the watchful eyes of authorities dictating fates. Amidst this, a covert resistance emerges, daring to defy and dismantle the status quo, embodying the novel's core themes of rebellion and resilience.

Through a blend of suspense, intrigue, and fiction, Paul Michael Peters dissects themes of love, faith, family, power, and control. This narrative compels readers to question their realities. "Right Hand of the Resistance" is an exploration of human extremes, delivering a narrative that resonates deeply with our contemporary challenges while hinting at ominous futures.

COMBUSTIBLE PUNCH

Rick Philips isn't a fighter—but he is a survivor.

Haunted by memories of a high school shooting, not even the bottle can wash away the gnawing guilt and creeping feelings of inadequacy that batter Rick's conscience daily.

His life has been a mess of broken marriages, writer's block, terrible choices, and the morbid pity of others. When he meets Harriet at a writer's conference, the record doesn't scratch as he falls back— only this time, he may not get up.

Harriet Bristol Wheeler is a dark temptress—and self-confessed serial killer.

INSENSIBLE LOSS

If you had the chance to live forever, would you take it?

2053: An old man, Viktor Erikson, lies on his deathbed. Alone and with no known relatives, he is tended to by Olivia, a nurse. He has only one request: that she reads to him.

The request is not unusual, but the battered, leather-bound tome she must read is no ordinary book. Written in 1839, it chronicles the discovery of the fountain of youth by Morgana de la Motte—and Viktor Erikson.

What starts off as a swashbuckling adventure on the high seas in search of riches and eternal life soon transforms into something quite different: a clash between two personalities bound by love and deceit, locked together by a terrible burden of necessity.

THE SYMMETRY OF SNOWFLAKES

Hank Hanson's family is not only blended; it's pulverized by the weight of its own perfect symmetry.

To the casual outsider, Hank Hanson's life might seem idyllic. As a successful businessman on the verge of a major business deal and an all-around good guy, few get close enough to see the troubled soul underneath his open face.

The product of a family fractured many times over by his parents' multiple remarriages, Hank spends his Thanksgivings running a miserable, thankless gauntlet of visiting multiple family members.

One Thanksgiving, he takes an unscheduled detour and meets Erin Contee, a woman who might just be too good for him—but at the same time, perfect. As the two grow closer together, Hank believes he has finally found the missing piece in his fragmented life.

MR. MEMORY AND OTHER STORIES OF WONDER

Uttering the name Mr. Memory evokes the live performances and talk show appearances when he would impress the world with his abilities of recollection. His clarity of remembrance has kept listeners captivated for days while sharing the adventures of his life. In this collection of short stories, we learn the truth about Mr. Memory, the fantastic gone unseen, and a world of wonder which can inspire us to believe.